The
MOST
Perfect Thing
in the
UNIVERSE

The
MOST
Perfect Thing
in the
UNIVERSE

Tricia Springstubb

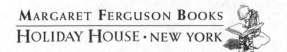
MARGARET FERGUSON BOOKS
HOLIDAY HOUSE · NEW YORK

The publisher wishes to thank Paul Sweet, Department of Ornithology
Collections Manager at The American Museum of Natural History,
for his expert help.

Margaret Ferguson Books
Copyright © 2021 by Tricia Springstubb
All Rights Reserved
HOLIDAY HOUSE is registered in the U.S. Patent and Trademark Office.
Printed and bound in February 2021 at Maple Press, York, PA, USA.
www.holidayhouse.com
First Edition
1 3 5 7 9 10 8 6 4 2
Library of Congress Cataloging-in-Publication Data
Names: Springstubb, Tricia, author.
Title: The most perfect thing in the universe / by Tricia Springstubb.
Description: First edition. | New York : Margaret Ferguson Books/Holiday House,
[2021] | Includes bibliographical references. | Audience: Ages 9 to 12.
Audience: Grades 4–6. | Summary: Unlike her adventurous
ornithologist mother, shy eleven-year-old Loah prefers a quiet life at
home with no surprises until her mother's expedition to the Arctic
tundra to study birds turns dangerous and Loah, alone at home,
discovers her own courage.
Identifiers: LCCN 2021003233 | ISBN 9780823447572 (hardcover)
ISBN 9780823450596 (ebook)
Subjects: CYAC: Mothers and daughters—Fiction.
Adventure and adventurers—Fiction. | Birds—Fiction.
Classification: LCC PZ7.S76847 Mr 2021 | DDC [Fic]—dc23
LC record available at https://lccn.loc.gov/2021003233

ISBN: 978-0-8234-4757-2 (hardcover)

For anyone who's ever longed for a nest, or wings, or both

It may be hard for an egg to turn into a bird: it would be a jolly sight harder for it to learn to fly while remaining an egg.

—C. S. Lewis

CHAPTER ONE

Loah Londonderry lived in a house with three chimneys and one alarmingly crooked turret. Built of mud-colored stone, the house sat in a small, dark forest of tall, looming trees. *Spooky* was the general opinion. Classmates from town, who no doubt lived in tidy homes with trim lawns, dared one another to spy through the windows. More than once, Loah had looked up from her laptop to see a pair of wide eyes staring at her. Loah would give a timid wave. The child would flee.

Loah herself was the least spooky person you could imagine. She was short and stout and shy, with curly brown hair and a left eye that wandered. She lived in the house with her mother, Dr. Anastasia Londonderry, and with the Rinkers, who took care of her when her mother was away, which was often. Dr. Londonderry was an ornithologist specializing in birds of the Arctic tundra. Not many species of birds lived there to begin with, and the ones that did were having a terrible time. Ground that had been frozen solid for tens of thousands of years was rapidly thawing and shrinking. Try to imagine helplessly watching your home disappear before your eyes, and you'll have an idea how the Arctic tern, spoon-billed sandpiper, and gyrfalcon feel.

Loah's mother could not single-handedly stop climate change, but she was a tireless, determined woman, and she did all she could to help the birds. She gave lectures. She wrote books. She went on numerous expeditions sponsored by the university where she was a professor. When she came home, she described her adventures to Loah: Navigating thick fog in small, flimsy planes. Sleeping in tents on rocky ground while wolves howled. Scaling cliffs. Eating lichens for breakfast and dried caribou meat for dinner. Dr. Londonderry would describe calving glaciers and fickle winds. Hungry bears. Killer whales.

Torture, in Loah's opinion.

Loah was a homebody. She didn't take after her mother or her father, who'd died before she was born, in a horrible mountain-climbing accident she didn't want to hear about, thank you. Loah would never climb a mountain, not if she could help it. Both feet on level ground was her motto. Her favorite activities included knitting, doing home repairs, and watching old episodes of *One and Only Family*.

Actually, she didn't love doing home repairs. Does anyone? Yet she did love her home, the nest she'd lived in for her entire eleven and a half years, and when you love something, you take care of it.

It was late June, the beginning of summer vacation, which meant she got to be home every day. This morning she woke to hear birdsong pouring through the open windows. Loah's parents had bought the property not for the house but for the trees, which were home to countless birds. ("We got it for a song," her mother would say with a warm, wry smile.) The birds serenaded Loah as she walked along the hallway with its peeling wallpaper, to the bathroom with its unreliable plumbing, down the staircase with its faded carpet of cabbage roses (which resembled, if you looked at them the right way, cheery pink faces), across the entry hall with its stag-head chandelier (not a real stag head, thank goodness), and along another dim corridor to the kitchen, where the floor was checkered black-and-white tile and the Rinkers' E-Z Boy recliners took up much of the space.

Loah looked out the window. The summer morning was fresh and blue, and the birds were jubilant. Actually, they were always jubilant in the morning, but today they were absolutely fizzy with joy. If you've ever shaken up a pop bottle, then unscrewed the cap? That kind of joy. Along with her team, Dr. Londonderry had been on her current Arctic expedition for fifty-seven days (Loah was definitely counting), but she was due home the day after tomorrow. Somehow, the birds seemed to know. Dr. Londonderry was their hero, after all. Their champion.

Loah herself had mixed feelings about birds. Ask her to name her favorite animal, and she would say cat, which was too bad for her, since cats are the number one predator of songbirds and under no circumstances was she allowed to have one.

Not to mention, birds were the reason her mother had been away for fifty-seven days and counting.

This morning, though, Loah and the birds were united in happiness. Soon, she and the Rinkers would drive to the airport, where her mother would sail through the gate in her all-weather jacket and hiking boots. When Loah hugged her, a hug that would go on for a long time, she'd smell of moss and midnight sun. Back home, they'd sit side by side in the house's library, eating sunflower seeds (Loah had already set them out on a little table) while Dr. Londonderry typed her expedition notes (using nine and two-thirds fingers, since she'd lost the tip of one to frostbite) and Loah worked on a knitting project. They'd eat their meals outside beneath the trees, which Dr. Londonderry always rejoiced to see after the tree-less tundra. She'd twist her little red wooden bird call, and a black-capped chickadee would fly down to take a sunflower seed from her hand.

At night, Loah's mother would tuck her in, then sit beside the bed. Outside, the screech owls would call back and forth. Often, Loah would wake to find her mother still there, watching her sleep. Mama would smile and put a finger to her lips, and Loah would drift back into contented dreams.

Loah had been counting the days. Now she was counting the hours. Her mother had promised not to go away again till next spring. Long, lovely months stretched ahead.

Standing by the kitchen window, she watched Miss Rinker prowl the yard with her scythe, looking for weeds to chop down. (If you're unsure what a scythe is, look up the Grim Reaper.) Meanwhile, Miss Rinker's brother, Theo, tenderly tended the hummingbird feeder. Both Rinkers were old, scrawny, and white as napkins. Theo was as delicate as Miss Rinker was tough. Her dentures didn't fit right, and when she wore them her upper lip was always slightly raised, as if she had to sneeze. Miss Rinker refused to get new ones, though. Thrift and sacrifice—that was *her* motto.

The phone on the counter began to ring, but Loah ignored it. Shy as she was, she didn't like talking to people in general, and talking to a disembodied voice was even worse. She opened the refrigerator and peered in, hoping to find something good to eat. In vain. Miss Rinker shopped at Bargain Blaster, where the food was cheap and weird. Thrift and sacrifice!

The phone persisted.

Was it Loah's imagination, or did the birds suddenly grow quiet?

She turned toward the phone and the ringing stopped. When she turned away, it began again.

It was not Loah's imagination. The birds had hushed. Only the mourning dove gave its mournful call. *Ah-coo-coo-coo...*

Loah crossed the room, recognized the number displayed, and gleefully seized the phone.

"Mama!"

"Sweetie!" said Dr. Londonderry. "I'm so glad you picked up."

Loah's heart did a cartwheel. Maybe her mother was about to surprise her! Maybe she'd left the field early and was already at the airport.

"Where are you?" she asked.

CHAPTER TWO

Dr. Londonderry's voice came and went. It sounded as if she were in a wind tunnel. "Just as we were packing up . . . something extraordinary . . . changed everything. . . ."

Loah's excitement began to fade.

"Are you outside?" she asked. "Is there a storm?" The tundra was not supposed to have storms in summer.

"This weather . . . warmest I've ever experienced . . . and the winds . . ."

There was a great deal of static. Loah gripped the phone, waiting for her mother's voice to return. When it did, she could not believe what she heard.

"Incredible news . . . your namesake . . ." Dr. Londonderry's voice was always squeaky but now it pitched even higher. ". . . hardly wait to tell you!"

Holding the receiver, Loah crossed the room and leaned her forehead against the window. Miss Rinker vigorously swung her scythe. Theo poured fresh water into a birdbath. They both looked so normal, so untroubled, it was hard to believe they existed in the same universe as she did at that moment. She chose her next words cautiously.

"Mama, the connection is so bad, I thought you said something about a loah bird."

"Yesterday the weather was calm, and I was taking one last reading of CO_2 levels on a fell-field of exquisite little sedges and wildflowers, when I heard the sweetest, shyest call. I looked up and to my astonishment..."

Her voice cut out again.

"Mama! Mama?"

"...fumbled for my camera...disappeared behind a pingo..."

Loah spun away from the window. The last reported sighting of a loah bird, by amateur birders on a cruise ship, had been eleven and a half years ago. Before that, nobody had seen one for over thirty years. The cruise ship sighting didn't count, not with the scientists who kept track of these things. The International Union for Conservation of Nature still classified the loah as in grave danger of being extinct.

"...that unique streak of gold on her alula...not the bright yellow of a goldfinch or the gaudy gold of a meadowlark, but a color deeper and richer..." Dr. Londonderry's voice squeaked with emotion. "Headed due west, toward the coast. It's late but still nesting season...clutch always small, no more than three eggs, always so vulnerable, and now with these conditions..."

If her mother had really, truly spied a loah, it was a mind-boggling discovery. These days no good news came out of the Arctic, which was warming at twice the rate of the rest of the globe. (Loah knew all about this and, if you asked, could also define *fell-field*, which means a rocky slope covered with low-growing plants; *pingo*, which is a dome-shaped hill of permafrost; and *alula*, which is a digit on the upper edge of a bird's wing used to fine-control flight.) Finding a creature everyone feared was lost forever would be a bright ray of hope in a long dark night.

"Sweetie!" said her mother. "My heart is singing like a nightingale!"

Loah's own heart plunged like a diving duck. She tried to brace for what was coming.

"It should just be a week," her mother said. "Well, realistically two, maybe three, but no more, I promise. Thank goodness I have leg bands, the digital scale, and, just in case, my incubation equip—"

Crash.

"Mama? Mama, are you there?"

"One second, sweetie." There were thudding, scraping sounds, as if her mother were engaged in a great struggle. At last she spoke again. "Not to worry. The Jeep door blew open but I...Oh for heaven's sake, what's this in my hair?" She laughed. "Dried caribou dung?"

You're supposed to come home. Loah swallowed back the words.

Her mother was saying how the bird's survival could provide crucial clues to helping other birds of the biome, not to mention spark funding for more research, not to mention...

Loah could barely listen. Disappointment overwhelmed her. She sank down on Theo's E-Z Boy.

"Are you sure you saw it?" she asked. "Loahs are so small and unremarkable."

"Ninety-nine percent sure. Her call—our only recordings of it are faint and scratchy, but I recognized it." Her mother imitated it. What she described as a sweet, shy song actually sounded more like someone wheezing with a chest cold.

"Did you get in touch with Dr. Whitaker?" He was her mother's boss at the university's Department of Mammalogy and Ornithology. Dr. Whitaker and Dr. Londonderry did not always see eye to eye, to put it mildly, but it was her job to report to him.

"Whit? That pessimist. I know exactly what he'd say." Dr. Londonderry pitched her voice low and ponderous. "Didn't get photos? No recording? Pardon the pun, Ana, but you're on a wild-goose chase. With our limited resources we can't—" A burst of static. "Besides, he's away on his own trek to Costa Rica this summer. I told the rest of the team to go ahead without me. They—"

"Wait." Loah sat up straight. "You're staying on alone?"

Another burst of static. The only words Loah caught were "increase in predators" and "time . . . of the essence."

"Mama," she said. "Are you sure this is a good idea?"

The phone crackled.

"I think this may be a bad idea. Actually, I'm sure it is. Mama?"

There was another crackle, a cry of ". . . love . . . so much! . . . ," and then nothing. Loah gripped the dead phone.

"Please change your mind," she begged. When there was no reply, she whispered, "Please be careful."

"Ahem."

Miss Rinker stood in the kitchen doorway. How long had she been there?

"My mother . . . ," said Loah. She got up and set the receiver back. Outside, not a single bird sang. "She has to . . . to unexpectedly extend her expedition."

Miss Rinker's upper lip lifted, revealing her oversized dentures. She looked about to sneeze. Or snarl.

"Your mother is a flighty woman," she said.

Did Miss Rinker mean this as a joke? If so, it would be the first joke Loah had heard her make in eleven and a half years. She tried to reply, but her voice, like the phone, had gone dead.

CHAPTER THREE

Loah hated to cry, but when it was absolutely necessary, she preferred to do it in private. The house had one place where nobody would look for her. She was forbidden to go there, and, obedient as she was, she almost never did.

She stumbled along the upstairs corridor, past the many unused bedrooms. (Miss Rinker and her brother slept in two rooms in the attic, which was uncomfortably cold in winter and unbearably hot in summer. Perfect, in Miss Rinker's view.)

A door at the very end of the corridor was shut, as always. Behind this door was the staircase leading to the turret. The turret was a precarious structure. It appeared to be an afterthought, as if the builder had decided to stick it on at the last minute, using inferior glue. Miss Rinker disapproved of the turret. She considered it frivolous, impractical, and probably unsafe, since the stonework was deteriorating. Loah was never to climb its stairs.

Loah had to tug hard to get the door open, then push hard to close it behind her. The forbidden staircase spiraled up and out of sight. Sinking onto the bottom step, she let herself cry. She was an explosive, messy crier. A water balloon hitting a sidewalk, that's what Loah's crying was like.

Mothers were supposed to come home. Even birds knew that. Birds were wonderful parents, as her very own mother had taught her. Building nests with twigs or mud, lichen or moss, spider silk or snakeskin, or sometimes with their own saliva. Laying their eggs and then sitting on them for weeks at a time, in every kind of weather. Finding their chicks seeds or insects or, in the case of raptors, small rodents, amphibians, or other creatures, which they tore into tiny, digestible pieces, which was so disgusting but also kind of lovable. Birds never abandoned their nestlings, if they could help it.

Loah's mother would make a very bad bird.

Loah rested her head against the cold stone wall and let loose with another loud, messy sob. She understood how important her mother's work was. She did. She truly did. If anyone in the world was proud of Dr. Anastasia Londonderry, it was Loah.

But she had a bad feeling, and not only because she was so disappointed and hurt. The tundra could be dangerous, even in summer. The terrain was uneven and boggy, making it easy to sprain an ankle or fall into icy water. It was plagued by biting insects. Global warming made everything highly unpredictable. What had her mother said about the predators? And going alone! She'd never done that before. It was against all expedition rules.

In the tundra, even satellite phones didn't always work, and Mama often forgot to recharge hers. There was no telling when they'd be able to talk again. Loah gave an even louder sob.

Hissss.

She bolted upright. What in the world was that? She held

perfectly still, listening. There it was again—a raspy sound, like someone dislodging something from a throat.

A dusty, mummified throat.

Quietly, Loah rose to her feet. Looking up, she saw nothing. A dark, dank nothing. She tried to tell herself it was the wind between the old crumbling stones. Except there was no wind.

Now she heard it again, closer this time.

She yanked on the door. It refused to budge.

Fear can sometimes endow a person with superhuman strength. This, however, was not Loah's experience. Fear made her go as weak as a pimply, just-hatched bird.

She whimpered. When she tried again, the door took pity and opened. Out in the corridor she leaned against the wall. What had just happened? Should she tell Miss Rinker? No, she'd only scold Loah for going near the turret. She'd say Loah was being hysterical and then make her drink warm milk.

Loah shut the door and, still hiccupping (she always hiccupped after she cried), hurried down the hallway to the safety of her own room. On the wall above her bed hung a framed print of a female loah bird. She was a tiny creature, weighing less than an ounce, with a head barely bigger than a hazelnut. Except for that streak of gold on her wing, her feathers were the color of dingy snow.

"It's all your fault she's not coming home," Loah accused the picture.

Which, unsurprisingly, did not reply. Loah sank onto her bed. On the nightstand was a photo of her and Mama. Mama was a small, plain woman, just the way Loah was a small, plain girl, but in this picture, with her arms around Loah and her chin resting on Loah's head, she looked radiant.

Holding her breath to stop the hiccups, Loah pulled what was left of her old baby blanket out from under her pillow. She'd mended it many times, but by now it was little more than a scrap of wool with a silky edge. She was rubbing that edge against her cheek when someone knocked on the door.

"Come in, Theo."

(It had to be him. Miss Rinker never knocked.)

"Look here." Theo tiptoed in, pulling a bag from under his shirt.

Gummy worms, their favorite. Miss Rinker—surprise, surprise—did not approve of candy, so Loah and Theo had to sneak. She chose a red-green one, Theo a yellow-orange. They ate solemnly, without speaking. Loah's mouth filled with rubbery sweetness.

"I'm sorry your mama's not coming home." Theo's hair was white as milkweed down. He cupped her hand in his old, spotty one. "I'm sure she would if she could."

Theo was so kind. Loah's mother *could* come if she chose, but he'd never say that.

"We'll just have to keep the nest warm till she gets here," he said.

Loah smiled. Theo was as much a homebody as she was. He set another gummy worm on her pillow, rocked back and forth a few times, and launched himself upright. Loah listened as the hallway floorboards creaked beneath his feet. Step, step, stop. Step, step, stop. Had he always moved so slowly?

Loah curled up with her baby blanket. Crying took it out of her, and she dozed off till a noise woke her. An odd, woody *thunk*. She sat up, listening, and heard it again, distant but distinct, like a buried heart. What was it? Her own heart raced.

Loah's heart, unlike the rest of her, was very athletic.

CHAPTER FOUR

The next day, no part of Loah felt right. Not her heart, not her head, not a single part. To keep from thinking about her mother, she busied herself with home repairs. Dr. Londonderry, accustomed to the spare rigor of an Arctic field station, tended to overlook problems like leaky faucets, cracked windows, and dubious electrical wiring. Theo was officially in charge of home repairs, but he was old and so was the house, and since time only runs forward, not back, they both just kept getting older. Loah would have died rather than hurt Theo's feelings, so she tried to do things surreptitiously, replacing a lightbulb here and tightening a loose screw there. It was hard to keep up, though, even with the small things. Big things like the crooked turret—well.

Loah had been hoping that when Mama got home, she could be convinced to get to work saving their own habitat.

Now Loah carried her Godzilla Glue and a broken cereal bowl (Theo had dropped it on the kitchen tiles) down the corridor to the house's library. The shelves overflowed with books on birds. Her mother had written many of them, including the one she was best known for, *The Egg: Nature's Greatest Feat of Engineering.* On the cover was a quote from someone named Thomas Wentworth Higginson: "I think, that, if required, on pain of death, to name instantly the most perfect thing in the universe, I should risk my fate on a bird's egg."

Loah set the broken bowl on her mother's desk, which was awash with a sea of journals, papers, unopened mail, and books; baggies containing feathers, eggshells, or bird poop; three pairs of binoculars; the red wooden bird call; and more papers, invitations to speak, thank-yous for speaking, awards, and certificates Mama never bothered to hang and had probably forgotten she ever received. On the very edge, lined up like dominoes, stood Loah's framed school photos, in which, year after year, her mouth frowned and her eye wandered.

In the center sat their other landline phone. This one was programmed with Dr. Londonderry's satellite phone number, which Loah was only to call in case of emergency.

Sitting down in her mother's chair, Loah absently reached for a shard of bowl and—*ouch!* A bright drop of blood bloomed on the tip of her finger. The sight of blood always made Loah woozy. She really, truly preferred blood to stay inside, where it belonged. She abandoned the bowl, wrapped her finger in a tissue, and went to the window seat, where her books from the public library were neatly stacked. She discovered one she hadn't read, a biography titled *Ferdinand Magellan: Circumnavigator of the Globe.*

Loah knew about the Magellanic penguin, so she'd been curious. Now as she read, she discovered that the bird was named for a sixteenth-century explorer in search of a route to the East Indies. Magellan was the hopeful sort, but things went all wrong. He ran out of supplies, and his men began dying of starvation, thirst, and various horrible diseases. Did Ferdinand Magellan turn back? He did not.

Ferdinand Magellan was making Loah nervous. Skipping to the book's end (something she never did), she read how he got mixed up in a tropical-island feud and wound up dead. His crew, what was left of it, forged on until, to their own surprise, they had sailed all the way around the world.

What to make of this? Magellan had led an expedition that discovered how immense the earth really was, not to mention proved that it was round, but only by accident. Plus, he'd gotten himself killed before it was over and missed out on most of it. For a great hero, he didn't seem to know what he was doing half the time.

She thought of her mother, alone at the top of the world. Which was so upsetting she slapped the book closed, stuck it under her arm, and went outside.

The yard was cool and leafy. Dr. Londonderry loved the trees because they sheltered the birds and sequestered carbon, but Loah loved the trees for themselves. A tree never went anywhere. It was always where you expected. It lost its leaves, but never its courage, and steadfastly grew new ones year after year. Try to name another living thing more patient and loyal than a tree, and you will fail.

Yet today Loah wandered among them like a ship lost at sea. She circumnavigated the mud-brown house. She peered up at the turret, with its two narrow windows (one had a broken pane) and its roof shaped like a witch's hat. Sunlight hit the windows and turned them white, like the eyes of the very old dog who slept all day in a corner of the town hardware store.

Did something flicker behind the glass?

Bony fingers clamped her shoulder. Loah spun around with a startled cry. Miss Rinker frowned at her.

"You're brooding again," she accused.

"No," said Loah, who knew too well Miss Rinker's cure for brooding. She held up *Ferdinand Magellan*. "I'm reading."

Miss Rinker took the book and skimmed the first page. Her lip curled. Her dentures glinted. She handed it back, saying, "Explorers! All they do is discover things that were already there."

This was true. But was it possible to discover something that *wasn't* there?

"What you need is exercise. A vigorous walk or a punishing bike ride."

"But . . . it's so hot. And sunlight causes cancer."

No use. Miss Rinker produced a tube of sunscreen. Also, her latest Bargain Blaster find: a metal water bottle that said THANKS FOR BEING YOU on its side.

(As if a person has a choice! Who else could you be, like it or not?)

CHAPTER FIVE

Loah's plan was to pedal out of sight, find a shady place to sit for an hour, then ride back. She put the water bottle in the mesh pocket of her photo-realistic snowy owl backpack (a birthday gift from her mother), snapped on her helmet, and wheeled her bike into the road.

Where a car, engine idling, sat in front of the house. The car had an official-looking seal emblazoned on its door. Behind the wheel, a man in a red baseball cap was furiously writing on a clipboard.

Loah hesitated. Should she ask him what he was doing? See if he needed assistance?

Probably. But remember how much Loah hated talking.

Instead she quickly pedaled away, and before long she realized that the day wasn't hot. It was breezy and mild, the kind of summer day that many people call perfect. The perfume of roses and lilies wafted from gardens, and sprinklers shot up rainbows. Leaves flickered and glowed as if the trees were thinking happy thoughts. Something about the day urged her on, and she kept riding.

Loah stopped thinking about her mother. She stopped thinking about the turret. She stopped thinking about anything whatsoever and watched a red-tailed hawk trace circles against the blue sky. She stood on her pedals to climb a hill. She turned off the main road and onto a smaller one that twisted and turned between green-gold fields. When she reached a fork, she hesitated. Should she turn around? She'd already gone much farther than she'd meant to, on roads that were unfamiliar. She was—she smiled to realize it—acting like a fearless, foolish explorer, off to discover wonders that might or might not be there.

The road on the left, she thought. Just a little bit farther.

She hadn't gone far at all when she hit the brakes. At the foot of a dirt driveway, an angry mob of handwritten signs shouted warnings.

KEEP OUT

PRIVATE PROPERTY

ATTACK DOG ON DUTY

TRESPASSERS WILL BE PROSECUTED OR WORSE

That last one was riddled with round holes.

A small boy with spiked-up hair the green of a monk parakeet rushed into the road.

"I hate you!" he hollered over his shoulder. "I hate your face! I hate you so bad I could kill you!" He skidded to a halt, spun around to face the way he'd come, and crossed his arms on his scrawny chest. "Try to get past me! Just try!"

Following his gaze, Loah saw a girl almost hidden by the signs. Thin, with colorless hair and flat, dark eyes, she looked about Loah's age. A beat-up, bulging backpack drooped from her shoulders. She wore rolled-up jeans, and her T-shirt was too faded to make out the picture on it. The toe poking out her sneaker wiggled, the only sign of life.

Behind the girl, the dirt driveway sloped upward, then dropped out of sight. Meadow grass and wildflowers blanketed the hill. It would have been a lovely, peaceful spot, except for those furious signs, the hollering boy, and the flat-eyed girl. None of this was Loah's business. Whatsoever. Except that, when she looked again, she saw that the girl's eyes were red. She'd been crying. Loah hooked her kickstand down. She slid her snowy owl backpack off and hugged it to her chest.

"Are you—" she began, but the boy suddenly charged her, snatched the backpack from her arms, and put it on. He strutted around triumphantly.

"Can't you read?" He pointed at the sign that said TRESPASSERS WILL BE PROSECUTED OR WORSE. "You ever heard of buckshot?"

Loah had, but only in books set in pioneer days.

"I—I'm not on your property," she said. "I'm on a public road. And I thought . . ." She looked at the girl, who rubbed her eyes with the heel of her hand and swiped her nose on the hem of her T-shirt, then once again went still. "I mean, is everything okay? I thought you might be in some kind of trouble."

The boy laughed. "Us Smiths *make* trouble, birdbrain!"

Being teased was nothing new to Loah. She was used to whispering and snickering. At school she'd been called Haunted House Girl. Also Googly-Eye Girl, as well as other names not worth mentioning. She'd been asked if she'd ever considered going on a diet. Usually she hunched her shoulders and walked away with as much dignity as she could muster. She'd gotten pretty good at it.

But now she wanted her backpack.

Also. Also, there was something about this girl. Who was she, anyway? She didn't go to Loah's school. She was silent as an egg, but things were going on inside her. Somehow, Loah could tell. Inside the girl was a commotion, a hubbub of feelings tumbling around. The girl kept quiet, but her toe wiggled, as if trying to send Loah a signal. As if she was sure Loah would reply.

Loah drew a breath.

"Actually," she heard herself say, "if you compare the ratio of brain weight to body weight, birds have bigger brains than we do. Their brains have significantly more neurons than primate brains of the same mass. So *birdbrain* may be a compliment."

The corners of the girl's mouth quirked up. Loah smiled back.

"Give me a break," said the boy.

But now he lost some steam. He slid a look toward the girl, checking to see what she was thinking. Big sister and little brother, thought Loah. He took a long drink of THANKS FOR BEING YOU water and wiped his mouth with the back of his hand. Loah noticed that, on the bottom of the sign saying KEEP OUT, a different hand had written *Keep in, you weirdos.*

Weirdo was one of the insults Loah had gotten good at ignoring.

The girl's toe wiggled again.

"Is your house over the hill?" asked Loah. "It reminds me a little of my house. I mean, of course I can't *see* your house, but that's my point, in a way. My house is hidden, too, only by trees. My mother loves trees. Well, I do, too. Though it's very nice out here, with all the unobstructed sky."

Parakeet Boy stared, then laughed. The girl's smile grew. A small, happy silence opened out, and then Loah heard what sounded like *baaa baaa* on the other side of the hill. She looked up, expecting to see sheep. She saw nothing, but now, out of sight, a dog started barking. From the sound, it was approximately the size of a school bus.

A man's voice bellowed what sounded like *Squirrel*. The girl flinched and threw a nervous glance over her shoulder. How could a squirrel make someone so angry?

"That's it, possum butt," the boy told his sister. "You're in big trouble now."

"Shut up!" she said.

Loah's adventurousness, or whatever it was that had brought her out here, began to fade. A cat with a bird struggling in its jaws raced across the road and vanished in the tall grass. The man shouted again, and this time there was no doubt his fury was directed at a squirrel.

What was going on over that hill? Nothing good. The barking grew louder. Time to get out of here.

"Please." Loah tried to sound brave. In vain. "Give me my backpack."

Quick as could be, the girl darted forward, snatched it from her brother, and handed it to Loah. Their eyes met, and the girl's were no longer flat. Instead, they sparked. They flashed as if she and Loah shared a secret. A secret so secret Loah had no idea what it could be, and yet her heart quickened. The girl looked at her as if Loah had a surprise in her pocket or a trick up her sleeve.

People rarely, if ever, looked at Loah that way.

With a roar, an enormous dog crested the hill. For one impossible second it hung there in suspended animation, then hurtled toward them. Its cinder-block head was lowered. Its ears were flat. It wore a spiked collar. A cartoon dog, only three-dimensional.

Maybe your parent has advised you what to do in case you get lost, or a shady stranger offers you a granola bar, or some other emergency arises. Loah's mother had explained what to do should you come face-to-face with a polar bear:

Keep an eye on the bear at all times, though do not—repeat *not*—make eye contact. Draw yourself up as big as possible and say, in the sternest voice at your command, *Get out of here.*

Never scream, Dr. Londonderry cautioned. This scares predators and causes them to attack for sure.

Do not scream, Loah told herself. Do not . . .

Some advice is impossible to follow.

"No!" she screamed, shutting her eyes. "Stop! Help!"

"Bully!" The girl's voice was astonishingly loud. A scrabble of claws. A high-pitched doggy whimper. When Loah dared to look, she saw the dog—was it really named Bully?—flat on the ground, eyes upturned, meekly watching the girl.

"Thank you," Loah whispered.

The humiliated dog swiveled its eyes and growled deep in its throat.

The man on the other side of the hill continued to shout. Would he come hurtling into view next? Something told Loah the girl wouldn't be able to handle him the way she had Bully.

"Come on." The boy grabbed his sister's hand and tried to haul her up the driveway. "You better come now. Before you get in really big trouble." When the girl shook him off he latched back on. "Come on. You wanna make Mama cry?"

"Don't!" she said. "Don't even talk to me."

She looked past her brother to Loah, and Loah nearly said, *Hop on my bike. Come home with me.*

What? She must have lost her mind. She didn't know this girl at all, and even if she did, she could hardly bring her home. Miss Rinker would have a conniption. Plus, the girl's family, which included a man who sounded both dangerous and demented, would come after her, and then what? *Plus* plus, why should this girl, who'd never laid eyes on Loah before, expect anything from her? Either she was extremely desperate or she, too, was demented.

She didn't look demented, though.

Which left desperate.

Her brother began to whine and beg. By now, he actually looked scared. Loah almost felt sorry for him.

"Don't go," he said.

Did he mean the girl? Or Loah?

Before she could find out, Loah pushed off on her bike.

"I'm sorry," she said, and pedaled away.

CHAPTER SIX

The ride back is always shorter than the ride there. Usually this is just a matter of perception, but today it was a matter of Loah riding faster than ever before.

All her life, the sight of home had filled her with relief. The rest of the world was so often baffling or hurtful, but at home she could be herself. She could stop wondering what people thought of her, what unexpected thing might happen next, what she would fail at. At home she could feel safe.

Yet today when she saw the pointy roof of the turret poking through the trees, the usual happiness didn't lift her. Instead, she remembered what she'd forgotten while she was away: Mama was not coming home. Re-remembering was even more painful, like bumping a bad bruise.

As Loah wheeled her bike into the garage, a blue jay landed on the edge of the sagging gutter. It fixed her with a bright, beady eye, then gave an ear-splitting screech. Jays are crabby birds, always complaining about something, but this one seemed especially put out.

In the kitchen, Miss Rinker reclined in her recliner, listening to opera, which she adored. In opera someone is always suffering from a wasting disease, being run through by a sword, getting trampled by a wild bull, or dying of a broken heart. Loah hung her helmet and backpack on the hooks by the door. She was hoping to make it upstairs to her room without an interrogation, but no luck. Miss Rinker jolted her recliner upright. She wore her THIS IS WHAT FABULOUS LOOKS LIKE! apron, another Bargain Blaster find.

"You got overheated." Her eyes went to the backpack. "Where's your water bottle?"

How could Loah admit that a boy who, even counting his spiky monk-parakeet hair, barely reached her shoulder, had stolen it? Miss Rinker would order her to go back and get it.

"I . . . I gave it to a boy in need."

This wasn't a lie, really. (Loah never lied, not if she could possibly help it.) That boy and his sister *were* in need . . . of something. Miss Rinker's thick, curly eyebrows (the opposite of her thin, straight hair, as if two different hair-factories were at work inside her) went vertical. Loah felt a stab of guilt. Partly because she'd lost the new water bottle, but mostly because she'd failed to help that girl. Though what could she have done?

Frowning, Miss Rinker got up and slapped together a liverwurst sandwich. She poured a glass of milk.

"Eat your lunch."

The bread was slightly moldy and the glass not exactly clean—Miss Rinker, who did not believe in doctors, really needed a visit with the ophthalmologist—but Loah discovered she was starving. Discreetly, she cut away the mold and began to eat.

When Theo shambled into the kitchen, Miss Rinker made him a sandwich, too. Usually Theo's appetite was as good as Loah's, but now he only picked at the food. He looked paler than usual, but he told Loah a joke about a donkey and a rooster that cracked them both up. No one enjoyed Theo's jokes more than Theo himself. The gentle chuckling sound pebbles make when you cup them and shake them—that was what his laugh was like. Now he pushed his sandwich aside, cocked his head, and looked at Loah.

"What's different about you?"

"Different?" said Loah, mouth squishy with liverwurst. "Me? Nothing."

"Something." He pretended to examine her head, making her laugh.

"She's taken to charitable acts," said Miss Rinker. "Eat your lunch, Theo. You're looking peaked."

It was true. Even laughing hadn't put the color back in his cheeks.

"Miss Rinker?" Loah asked. "Did my mother happen to call while I was gone?"

Miss Rinker's look might have been sympathetic, had Miss Rinker believed in sympathy.

"Dr. Londonderry's got a one-track mind. Bird bird bird bird. If I were you, I wouldn't expect to hear from her anytime soon."

CHAPTER SEVEN

When Loah was little, she'd invented a game she called Egg. She'd curl up and pretend to be inside a shell. She'd close her eyes and imagine she was in a nest, tucked beneath the downy feathers of her parent bird. She'd do this in bed or in Theo's E-Z Boy or in any other place that was warm, cozy, and snug. Often she fell asleep.

Not much of a game, you may be thinking, and who could argue?

The only person she'd ever told about Egg was Theo. One day when she was six or so, he'd found her in his lounger, hugging her knees, chin to chest. If he'd been Dr. Londonderry, he'd have asked what was wrong. If he'd been Miss Rinker, he'd have marched her outside for fresh air and exercise.

But he was Theo, gentle, dovelike Theo, so he'd buttered a stack of saltines—buttered saltines were the Rinkers' idea of a big treat—and settled himself beside her. As they ate, Loah explained about Egg.

"Ah," he'd said, as if he knew just what she was talking about. As if he'd played that very game himself. The two of them sat quietly until, to Loah's surprise, he said, "When my sister was your age and I could barely walk, our mother gave us away to the orphanage."

Loah could not have been more shocked. Theo and his sister never talked about their past.

"I can't remember her. Our mother. But I remember the orphanage." He swept saltine crumbs into his palm. "Did you ever notice that, though it's cheap as can be, my thrifty sister never makes cabbage? That's because the orphanage served it to us every single day. It's a wonder we didn't turn into cabbages." He sighed. "We each got one blanket, so thin you could poke your finger through. Still, it wasn't so bad, because we were together, and she looked out for me night and day. Except for that time I came down with the fever. She couldn't protect me from that. Oof. I shivered and sweated and itched all over. My tongue swelled up like a sausage and I—"

Loah must have looked horrified, because Theo quickly took her hand in his, scattering cracker crumbs everywhere.

"I got better, as you can see," he said.

Loah had heard fairy tales about children abandoned in dark forests or sent to live with evil stepmothers, but she'd never imagined this could happen in real life, certainly not to anyone she knew, and especially not to Theo and Miss Rinker. She'd never even imagined them as children, let alone small, helpless orphans. Tears stung her eyes.

"It was mean of your mother to leave you," she whispered. "Very, very mean."

His face fell and he turned away. Loah bit her tongue, afraid she'd made him sad, but then he said, "There's no good in thinking that way. She did the best she could, as all mothers do."

Patience and kindness, that was Theo's motto.

He gave Loah another saltine and explained that nobody had adopted them, maybe because Miss Rinker vowed to murder any-one who tried to separate them. As soon as she was old enough to make her own way in the world, she and Theo said good riddance to the orphanage. They lived here and there, and did this and that.

His voice kept growing smaller, like a piece of paper being folded into a tiny square.

"It wasn't till we came here, and your mother—"

"She had no idea what she was doing," interrupted Miss Rinker. Who, they were startled to discover, had snuck up behind the lounger and now came around to face them. She clutched a dust-pan and broom, her knobby knuckles white. "Your father had died, and she was alone in the world. Alone with you. She advertised for a caretaker. When we came for the interview, she opened the door with you in her arms. Bawling! Red as a beefsteak and tight as a fist! I never saw a child who could cry as fiercely as you, before or since. Your poor mother was ready to drop."

Miss Rinker attacked the floor with her broom.

"She didn't know the first thing about babies. A feeling of security—that's what you wanted. I had to show her how to wrap your blanket neat and snug, and how to hold you with authority."

(It was the same baby blanket Loah still kept under her pillow.)

"You stopped crying, though you had the hiccups for the next hour." She swept ferociously, as if the floor had done something she could never forgive. "Then it was your mother's turn to bawl. With gratitude."

"My sister," Theo whispered in Loah's ear, "was pretty happy, too."

31

Miss Rinker set her hand in the small of her back. Some old people's eyes are always watery, but not Miss Rinker's. At that moment, though, they grew misty.

"So," Loah prompted, "you moved in here."

Miss Rinker dabbed her eyes with her apron, and for a second she seemed to wobble in her sturdy lace-up shoes. Loah could still, even now, years later, remember what Theo did next. He stood and took his sister's hand. He pressed it to his chest, making a second heart on top of his.

"We'd never lived anywhere that felt like a real, true home, before this." He smiled down at Loah, and then he winked. "We were eggs without a nest."

Loah jumped up and took his other hand. The lines in Miss Rinker's face softened. Someone younger and gentler stood there, someone capable of fear and sorrow.

"I'm so glad you came here," Loah blurted. "And I'm really sorry your mother abandoned you!"

Snap! The impenetrable Miss Rinker returned. She stepped backward, separating herself from Loah and Theo. It was then she said a horrendous, unforgettable thing.

"All mothers fail their children, some in small ways and others spectacularly."

Now and then, a person says something that sets you vibrating, as if their words are the wind, and you are a windchime.

Loah trembled.

"I'm sorry," said Miss Rinker, and for once in her life she did, truly, look sorry. "But it is the truth."

Miss Rinker was a firm believer in truth. Even if it hurt.

Especially if it hurt.

Though Theo took Loah outside, where she sat on the swing he'd hung from the sturdiest oak, and though he pushed her just the way she liked, medium-high and not crooked, and though he sang her a song about a man who had the sillies, and later took a drop of nectar from the hummingbird feeder and touched it to her lips—though Theo tried his best to comfort her, nothing could erase what Miss Rinker had said. Like a stain on her heart, Loah carried it around with her for days to come. Though eventually she stopped thinking about it, it never completely went away.

CHAPTER EIGHT

For the next few days, Loah spent most of her time in the library, sitting at her mother's desk. She knitted. She watched YouTube videos about reglazing cracked windows (dangerous) and repairing dry rot (inadvisable). She straightened the teetering piles of mail, and binge-watched *One and Only Family*, even though she knew most episodes by heart (actually, *because* she knew most episodes by heart—what is more comforting than the predictable?).

All the while, she kept one eye on the landline phone in the center of the desk. Watched pots don't boil, and watched phones don't ring. But no news was good news, right? She told herself that if something had gone wrong, her mother would have called. She definitely would have called.

One day, hungry, Loah left the library and went down the long corridor to the kitchen, where Miss Rinker's indignant voice made her stop outside the door.

"It's not just herself she's putting in danger. It's her child, too! Her one and only child."

"You can't blame a person for who she is," said Theo.

"I do blame her! I blame her completely and utterly! If something should happen to her, Loah would be an orphan!"

"She's always got us," said Theo quietly, which made his sister sputter something incomprehensible.

Loah stumbled back to the library.

You are probably thinking, Why didn't Loah just pick up the phone and call her mother? You would, wouldn't you? But the rule was *No phoning except in case of emergency*, and Loah respected rules. She'd found that sticking to the rules made life easier. The parts of life with no rules, or rules she couldn't understand—such as how to fit in and make friends at school—were confusing enough. When a straight, sure path was laid out for you, why not follow it?

But speaking of straight, sure paths: When she sat back down at her mother's desk, she found herself thinking again about the girl she'd met on that twisty back road. If the girl were a bird, she'd be an egret. Tall, narrow, watchful. What did her little brother mean when he said she'd make their mother cry? Making your mother cry was serious. Loah never had and hoped she never would.

The girl had been on the brink of something. When Loah came along, she'd been ready to step out into the dusty road. Where was she going, wearing that bulging backpack? Why was her little brother so upset? The more Loah thought about it, the more she became convinced that the girl was running away from home, and he was trying to stop her. Running away from home was unimaginable to Loah, who usually was running *toward* home, but when she remembered the menacing KEEP OUT signs, the slobbering dog, and the shouting man, she wondered if the girl had ended up running away after all, or if she'd turned around and trudged back over that hill.

Either choice was awful.

Loah had wanted to help her.

She still did.

Across the rubble of her mother's desk, Loah's school photos frowned at her. Why had Mama bought them? They were terrible pictures. One by one, Loah laid them facedown on the desk, then got up, clumped down the hall, crossed the entry hall beneath the stag-head chandelier, and picked up the mail that had fallen through the slot in the door. Sitting on the staircase, she was sorting through it when Theo came to tell her that he and Miss Rinker were going to town on errands. Did she want to come?

Loah traced a cabbage rose on the staircase carpet. She knew Theo wanted her to join them, but she just didn't have the heart for the Bargain Blaster today. As gently as she could, she said no thank you. Theo promised they wouldn't be long.

The mail was all junk except for one official-looking envelope from the city. She set it on the teetering pile on Mama's desk, then gathered her cell, receiver for the landline, and her laptop, and went outside. Sitting in the swing Theo had hung for her in the big oak, she clicked on *One and Only Family*. The show had gone off the air so long ago it was essentially prehistoric, the kind of show where mothers were forever icing cakes and fathers wore ties at the dinner table. No one was ever lonely or frightened for more than five minutes. Not even the family dog. She was deciding between the Great-Aunt Rosie surprise party episode and the one where the twins are born, when two girls turned into the driveway. They dropped their scooters in the gravel. Loah recognized them from school. They were good at sports and had long, flowy hair. Neither had ever paid any attention to Loah, and they didn't see her now as they crept giggling toward the house.

"Sooooooo spooky!"

"Haunted much?"

"Feel that chill in the air? That means paranormal activity!"

Loah, as you know, was accustomed to being teased. But these girls were making fun of her home, the place she loved best in the world. They were invading her territory.

"Look at that tower!" one of them said. "You just know it's full of bats and bones and—"

"It's a turret, not a tower!" The words leaped out of Loah, surprising her. "And you feel a chill because the trees cool the air, not because of ghosts."

The girls spun around, clutching each other.

"Eek!" squealed the blond one.

"You scared us silly!" squealed the other blond one.

"You already are silly," Loah said, surprising herself even further.

"Don't worry—we are *so* out of here!" Giggling like lunatics, tripping over each other, the girls grabbed their scooters and raced away.

Loah closed her laptop. Her heart was beating too fast. Those girls would undoubtedly tell all their friends how she'd scared them half to death. This would definitely add to her weirdo reputation. Yet she couldn't have stopped herself if she wanted to. Some other, unknown Loah had rushed forth, defending what she loved.

Then, just as her heart began to slow, with no warning whatsoever, as if an invisible hand had given it a shove, a roof slate broke loose. It slid down, clanged against the gutter, and plummeted to the ground. Those slates were heavy. Their edges were keen as ax blades. Miss Rinker said that if one struck you on the head or neck, it was curtains for you. (This was the kind of grisly fact Miss Rinker adored.)

If that slate had fallen moments earlier, the Scooter Girls might have been goners.

Loah could see the gap, just beside the turret, where the slate had broken off. The roof already leaked, so this was worrisome. Was the turret a little more crooked? And look at that broken windowpane! For a moment, she saw her home through the eyes of the Scooter Girls.

Spooky. Creepy. Haunted much.

The blank eyes of the turret windows stared back at her. She remembered the eerie hissing she'd heard when she'd sat at the foot of its winding steps. She'd tried to convince herself she'd imagined the sound, but now a spine-prickling chill made her jump off the swing. She wound her way among the trees to peer up the road toward town. Where were the Rinkers? Theo drove at the approximate speed of a Galápagos tortoise, but errands never took them this long. What if they'd had an accident? What if they were in an ambulance on the way to the hospital right now? Loah saw them on stretchers, eyes shut, heads turbaned in bloody bandages. What if they were hurt so badly that they . . . never returned?

When one thing in your life goes wrong, especially if that thing is not a thing at all but your mother, it's suddenly easy to imagine other bad things happening. Even if you are a person who mostly stays home and avoids bad things as much as possible. Maybe especially if you are.

A shadow darkened the sunlit road. Loah looked up to see what had caused it, but nothing was there. It was as if the sky had a slit, and whatever had cast the shadow had slipped through.

A car approached. The wrong car. It was the same car she'd seen parked in front of the house a few days ago. It slowed, then stopped. Out climbed a man carrying a clipboard and wearing a red baseball cap. He touched its brim and nodded at her.

"Is this your house? Is your mother home?"

CHAPTER NINE

Loah knew better than to admit she was alone, and yet, alone as she felt at that moment, the words spoke themselves.

"Not yet."

The man handed her a card: *Wayne J. Kipper, City Housing Inspector.*

"Wayne J. Kipper, City Housing Inspector," he said, as if she couldn't read. His chin wore either a terrible beard or a smear of butterscotch pudding. He gave a tight, all-purpose smile. "If she's not here, who's watching you?"

"I'm eleven and a half."

"I see. Mind if I have a quick look at the property?" Without waiting for a reply, he strolled up the gravel driveway. The birds, who'd been doing their usual chittering and chattering, grew quiet. A blue jay perched on the rim of a birdbath and fixed Inspector Kipper with its beady eye. He pushed back his red cap to peer up at the turret.

"Hmm." He made a note on his clipboard. "Hmm."

They were unfriendly *hmm*s. The jay squawked and looked at Loah as if asking her to do something. But the inspector was an official adult. Loah had defended her house against the Scooter Girls, but this was different. She took a deep breath.

"You are on my private property," she said. "Could you please explain your business. Please."

Inspector Kipper pointed. "That tower's angle of inclination is critical," he said.

"I don't mean to be rude, but it's a turret."

He was, she could tell, the kind of adult who filed anyone younger than sixteen in the same generic category: kid. But now he looked at her more closely.

"My niece has lazy eye, too. She wears a patch. You ever try a patch?"

"I'm sorry to correct you again, Inspector, but it's not called lazy eye. It's called amblyopia."

"Is that so?" He drew back, frowning. "Will Dr. Londonberry be back soon?"

"It's *derry*." All right—now she was losing her patience. "And not soon."

"Then I'll just have to go ahead with the on-site inspection." He pulled a phone from his pocket. "I'll be taking some snaps."

He strolled around, aiming his phone at the turret, the roof, the back steps, even the trees. He covered his clipboard with checkmarks. Something told Loah they were bad, not good, checkmarks. He wore a utility belt with an assortment of things attached: a flashlight, clippers, a canister of something. He stubbed his toe on the fallen roof slate and muttered darkly.

The birds were watching. They were always watching, of course, because birds are forever on the lookout for danger. They are experts at stealthy spying. A person with an untrained eye could be surrounded by dozens of birds and never guess. It's not as if birds, under normal circumstances, want anything to do with humans.

At last the inspector took off his cap and fanned his face

"Prior code inspections have been done from the street," he told Loah. "As is legal. Thank you for permission to do this on-site." The cap had left a dent all around his hair. In the middle, a bald spot shone like a large pink egg in a butterscotch-colored nest.

"Prior?" she said.

"This job," he said. "It's not easy. On a day-to-day basis, we get attacked by wasps and hornets. Chased by dogs. Bitten by vermin. Don't even get me started on homeowners who threaten us with bodily harm. One of my colleagues actually got chased off the premises with a load of buckshot." He pooched his lips. "In point of fact, being a housing inspector is a thankless job." He slowly shook his head. "But someone's got to do it."

"Do what?"

The birds began to show themselves. They hopped sideways on branches and peeked out from under shrubs, twisting their heads, flicking their tails. You probably already know that groups of birds have special names. There are gaggles of geese, murmurations of starlings, wisdoms of owls, exaltations of larks. In the oak where Loah's swing hung, an American crow sounded its warning *caw*. A group of crows is a murder.

"Do what?" Loah repeated.

The inspector turned his melancholy gaze on her. "How old did you say you are?"

"Eleven and a half."

"And you're here by yourself?"

Loah could have explained about the Rinkers, but they weren't any of this nosy man's business. She drew another breath. "Not at the moment," she said.

"There's been no progress on the violations." He tapped his clipboard. "When did you say your mother's coming home?"

The jay screeched. The inspector frowned and settled his cap low on his brow.

"I didn't say," Loah replied. "But she will! Come home."

His look was dubious. "When was the last time she had someone look at these trees?"

"I look at them every day."

"An expert, I mean. In point of fact, tree roots can totally mess up a sewer system, not to mention compromise a foundation. Especially an old one like this. In addition, all this shade is causing moss and fungal growth on the roof, which can lead to further deterioration. And see that branch right there? It weighs half a ton, easy. If that thing fell, it'd take out your tower."

"Turret," she whispered.

It was one thing to notice for yourself that your house could use tender loving care here and there. And there, too. It was a completely different thing for an inspector with a clipboard and a car emblazoned with an official seal to point this out in an unfriendly, slightly menacing way.

The birds flickered and fluttered, darting about. The crow gave a cry like a rusty hinge swinging in the wind. The inspector nervously fingered the canister hanging from his belt. What was in there? Loah drew yet another deep breath. Maybe the inspector didn't understand.

"My mother says trees are the best weapon against climate change," she said. "They pull carbon from the air and store it.

Humans are still trying to develop the technology to lock up carbon, but trees have been doing it for three hundred and fifty million years. In addition, trees capture particulate pollution." For someone who disliked talking, especially to strangers, this was an exhausting speech, but she managed to add, "Also, they are beautiful and noble."

"I thought your mother was a doctor. How does she know so much about trees?"

"She's an ornithologist."

"Hmm." He took off his cap again and scratched his sweaty bald spot. "Is that so."

A confusion of warblers, a quarrel of sparrows. You didn't need to be an ornithologist to understand the birds were sounding an alarm. Loah's mother said that even a bird the size of an olive would defend its territory.

"I suppose your mother likes birds, too," he said.

"Likes?" Loah blinked. "Birds are her life."

"Really?" He snickered. "Birds?"

The jay jetted down and grazed the top of his head. Blue jays are large for songbirds, and they can fly at up to twenty-five miles per hour. Their bills can crack acorns with absolutely no problem. In other words, you don't want a jay for your enemy.

Alarmed, the inspector waved his cap in the air. As if it were a matador's red cape and they were the bulls, more jays and a hairy woodpecker joined the attack, zeroing in on his bald spot. The inspector flailed. The birds shrieked. The cap flew.

"What the—"

He fumbled for the canister on his belt and managed to unhook it, but as he took aim, Loah lunged forward and knocked it away.

He stared in disbelief. "You shouldn't have done that, young lady!"

"Don't you dare hurt the birds!"

"Tell Dr. Londonberry she needs to contact my office immediately. She's ignored our notices long enough. Irresponsibility has consequences!" He charged down the driveway.

"Derry!" Loah ran after him with his cap. He grabbed it, then dived into his car and slammed the door. He rolled his window down.

"And tell her she better teach her daughter how to behave! Obstructing city business is punishable by law."

He jammed the cap back onto his head but not before Loah saw, with a small thrill, the beak-sized puncture in the middle of his bald spot.

"Till we meet again!" he said, and the car sped away.

Dizzy! The yard was dizzy with bright eyes and feathered breasts puffed with triumph. (In addition to lungs, birds have numerous air sacs.) Loah picked the canister up from the ground. THE TERMINATOR, said the label.

"We showed him," Loah told a tufted titmouse. It bobbed its tuft in agreement.

She hurled The Terminator into a trash can and collapsed onto a lawn chair, a little dizzy herself. As she tried to assess the situation, the thrill she'd felt soon gave way to fear and worry. Inspector Kipper disapproved of her mother, her house, her trees, and her birds.

Not to mention her.

Punishable by law was not a phrase that had ever been applied to Loah before, as you can probably guess.

What notices was he talking about? What consequences?

As Loah's head whirled, yet another question she couldn't answer presented itself. The family car hairpinned into the drive and came to an abrupt, juddering stop. Gripping the steering wheel, head barely visible above the dashboard, was Miss Rinker.

Where was Theo?

CHAPTER TEN

Slumped in the back seat, it turned out.

"He went down," Miss Rinker said. "In the Bargain Blaster checkout line. He knocked over a big display of beach balls."

When Loah opened the car's back door, Theo gave her a feeble smile.

"They bounced everywhere," he whispered. "I wish you could have seen it."

Loah tried to help him out, but his legs didn't want to move. At last she crouched, took his right shoe between her hands, and gently lowered it to the ground. He managed the left one on his own, then clutched her arm and hoisted himself up. The back of his head had a painful-looking bump.

"The Bargain Blasters called 911." Miss Rinker wore her going-to-town outfit: a sweater Loah had knitted (Miss Rinker had chosen the wool, which was so prickly it was like knitting a cactus) and a straw hat with a snow goose feather (a gift from Dr. Londonderry). Her hair had come loose from its bun and straggled over her shoulders like gray tentacles. "I told them he'd be fine, but they insisted. By the time the ambulance came, he was sitting up and making sense again. *See?* I said. *Much ado about nothing.*"

Miss Rinker, as you know, took a dim view of doctors. That time she was chopping vegetables and mistook her thumb for a baby carrot? That time her hammertoe hurt so bad she couldn't wear a shoe for a week? Even that time she tumbled off the stepladder and for an excruciating few minutes believed she was on a hard cot in the chilly, cabbagey orphanage? She refused to see a doctor. It was no surprise she hadn't wanted Theo to go to the hospital, and yet, as he leaned heavily against her, Loah worried that Miss Rinker had made the wrong decision.

Watching grown-ups make wrong decisions you are helpless to stop—this is one of the worst parts of being a child.

"We had to get home," Theo whispered. "To bring you your present."

"Present?" The Rinkers only gave presents at Christmas and birthdays, and then they were always socks or pajamas. Loah's worry deepened. "What present?"

"You'll see."

They made their halting way up the back steps (careful on the bottom one, which was rotting) and into the house. Loah guided Theo into his E-Z Boy while Miss Rinker wrapped ice cubes in a dish towel. Loah gently pressed them to the bump on his head as Miss Rinker made him drink some water.

"The present," Theo said in a raspy voice totally unlike his real, gentle one. "We need to give Loah her present."

Miss Rinker retrieved the Bargain Blaster bags from the car. She set them on the table and began pulling things out. Tins of sardines and jars of pickled vegetables. Paper napkins printed with storks carrying babies in pink and blue blankets. A stack of flat, unidentifiable squares so blindingly yellow they appeared radioactive.

Theo's eyes drifted closed. His skin was gray as an old athletic sock. What if he had a concussion? Weren't you supposed to keep the person awake? Weren't you supposed to ask him to name the current president of the United States?

"Are you sure he's all right?" Loah whispered to Miss Rinker.

"He lost his balance. He's very old, you know." He was younger than Miss Rinker, but arguing with her was as pointless as arguing with the sidewalk. "Theo." She touched his arm. "I'm about to give Loah her present."

It took him a moment to focus, but then he smiled at Loah. "We know you miss your mother. We want to cheer you up."

"And," said his sister, "give you something to think about beside yourself."

Miss Rinker opened the last bag. There couldn't possibly be a kitten in there, could there? (If this was *One and Only Family*, there would be. With a pink bow around its neck.)

Miss Rinker paused dramatically, then reached inside and pulled out a clear plastic bag containing . . . a goldfish. Which did not move, but hung in the water as if suspended from an invisible thread.

"Oh," said Loah. "Is it . . . is it alive?"

"It better be!" cried Miss Rinker. She tapped the bag and the fish flinched.

They'd also bought a Your First Fish Starter Set, complete with a bowl, sand, colored pebbles, a plant, fish food, and a small net. The instructions said to wash the bowl and pebbles, put the sand on the bottom, fill the bowl with water, add the special water conditioner, and then wait. Fish, the booklet said, were sensitive creatures. Changes of environment stressed them out. Loah felt a rush of sympathy. She followed the instructions carefully, ending by setting the plant at what she hoped was a comforting angle. She lowered the bag into the bowl and, once the temperature in the bowl and bag were the same, she released the fish into its new home. It did a single, cautious lap, then sank to the bottom of the bowl.

"He's shy," said Theo. "Like you."

"He's overcome," said Miss Rinker. "He can't believe his luck."

They beamed at Loah. Well, Miss Rinker, of course, didn't *beam*, but she did look pleased, which was rare enough. A lump formed in Loah's throat. The Rinkers were trying to make her happy. They knew she was upset about her mother, and they wanted to help. This was kind and good of them, but they'd gone about it in a totally wrong way. You can't pet a fish. You can't even touch it. The last thing a fish is going to do is curl up in bed with you like a kitten. Plus, this poor fish looked as if its days were numbered.

Loah swallowed around the lump. The Rinkers watched her eagerly. Disappointed as she was, she couldn't disappoint them. She bent over the bowl, where her fish wallowed in bewilderment.

"Hello," she said in what she hoped was a cheery voice. "Welcome to your new home! I hope you'll be happy here."

Maybe fish experts (otherwise known as ichthyologists) can tell if a fish is happy or sad, but Loah couldn't. She turned to Miss Rinker and Theo.

"Thank you," she said. "Thank you very much."

That night, while Theo napped in his lounger, Loah and Miss Rinker had barley soup and sardine sandwiches (which Loah hoped the goldfish didn't notice). Afterward Miss Rinker settled into her E-Z Boy and turned on the TV, which was approximately the size of a cereal box. She dialed the volume way up (hearing aids? Miss Rinker would not hear of them) and tuned in to a detective show. Before a single victim could be murdered or kidnapped, she was sound asleep, too, head back and mouth open like a baby bird.

Only now, when things were quiet, did Loah remember the housing inspector. What with Theo being hurt and the new fish, she'd temporarily forgotten all about Wayne J. Kipper. It was definitely too late to tell Miss Rinker now. Look how exhausted she was. This long, trying day had done her and Theo in. They didn't need anything more to worry about.

Loah tucked their Bargain Blaster blankets over them. Miss Rinker's had footballs and pennants. GO TEAM! it urged. Theo's had a herd of wild ponies galloping across a plain.

As she slowly climbed the steps to her room, she studied the carpet's roses, trying to see cheery, pink faces.

CHAPTER ELEVEN

If you've ever gone to a sleepover (Loah had not, of course), you know how much fun it is to stay up all night. The only downside is the next morning. You're zonked. The smallest thing makes you weepy or giggly. Or both at once. You feel as if you're poked full of holes. You're a colander and the world is pouring through you.

Thus Loah this morning. She'd taken forever to fall asleep, and when she did, she'd had bad dreams: Her fish inflated like an orange water balloon and popped. A slate slid from the roof just as Theo walked by and he crumpled into a heap (it was possible his head was chopped off, but even in a dream, Loah didn't have the courage to look). Just before she woke, she dreamed of a giant squirrel wearing a red cap and muttering, *There will be consequences.*

Loah was not used to feeling like a colander. She was more pot-like. She dragged herself from bed. She did her ocular exercises, which were as tedious as they sound. She pulled on shorts and a T-shirt. She dreaded going downstairs. She didn't want to tell Miss Rinker that she'd obstructed justice. She was afraid the fish actually might have died. She hated the thought of another day of endlessly waiting for Mama to call.

Down the stairs, beneath the stag-head chandelier, and into the kitchen, where, to her shock, Theo still lay in his E-Z Boy lounger. His wild-ponies blanket was still tucked over him, and he still wore yesterday's clothes. His soft milkweed hair was sweaty and matted against his skull.

Miss Rinker, busy at the stove, put a finger to her lips.

"You slept late," she accused.

She still wore yesterday's clothes, too. Her cactus sweater was buttoned wrong, and her cheeks had extra wrinkles. She must have slept down here last night, as well. She set a bowl of unsweetened oatmeal in front of Loah.

"Eat your breakfast, then off you go to the library. Your books are due."

"Miss Rinker," Loah began, but the old woman put her finger to her lips again.

As Loah obediently swallowed the awful oatmeal, Miss Rinker held up one of the blindingly yellow squares she'd bought at the Bargain Blaster. When she gave it a shake, it turned into a thin poncho with the word CREW stamped in giant letters on the back.

"I got five of them for two dollars," she said in a low, pleased voice. "There's a fifty percent chance of rain. This will keep you dry and make you visible to traffic."

She'd be visible to astronauts on the space station. Arguing with Miss Rinker was always a lost cause, though, and this morning, tired as she was, Loah didn't even try. She slipped the poncho over her head. She flapped her arms, certain she looked like a large, radioactive duck.

"Very nice," said Theo from his chair. Loah rushed to him.

"How do you feel?"

"Never better." He levered his lounger upright. But when he tried to stand, his head trembled like a flower on a fragile stem. Running his tongue over his lips, he sank back. "Maybe . . . maybe a bit more rest."

This was not right. Morning was Theo's favorite time. He was usually up with the birds, whistling his own tune.

"How is your fish?" he whispered.

Loah checked. The fish was still alive, though it didn't look very happy about it. She fed it then turned to Miss Rinker.

"I should stay home," Loah told her. "In case you need me."

"Need you?" Miss Rinker's eyes blazed. "My brother needs to rest, and I need to do my housework, and you need to return your library books before you get a fine. That's all the needing there will be, thank you."

"But—"

"You do remember who you're talking to, don't you, Loah Londonderry?"

Loah gathered up her library books. When she came back to the kitchen, she found Miss Rinker, hands clasped beneath her chin, hovering over her brother. *Old* was the first word that sprang to mind when you saw the Rinkers. But this morning, they looked beyond old. They looked as brittle as the pages of an ancient manuscript. Was it possible to age so much overnight? Some birds reach full maturity within two weeks of hatching. So maybe.

Loah took her snowy owl backpack from its hook. She put her books in and zipped it shut. Once again she remembered the inspector, but once again it was the wrong time for bad news.

"Goodbye," she said.

Neither of them seemed to hear.

She rode to town in slow motion, the poncho rippling around her. A passing car honked and a teenage boy yelled, "Hey, Crew! You forgot your boat!"

Her favorite librarian, the one with sparkly purple glasses, was at the desk. She admired Loah's poncho, then noticed *Ferdinand Magellan: Circumnavigator of the Globe* among the books she held.

"You're interested in explorers? Hang on!" She dashed off and returned holding a fat volume. "We just got this in."

Women Spacefarers, said the cover.

"I'm absolutely petrified of heights. I get terrible motion sickness. No way I could be an astronaut. I am to these women as a mouse is to a lion." The librarian's glasses twinkled like wishing stars. "But that's why we read, isn't it? To have the most hair-raising adventures while curled up on our own cozy couches. Or in my case, my dilapidated futon. So many things to discover! Infinite possibilities! A world of jaw-dropping wonders!" She blushed and gave an embarrassed laugh. "My boyfriend's always telling me I get too carried away."

Loah thought that if she ever had to get glasses, they would definitely be purple and sparkly.

"I'll take the book," she said. "Thank you."

Next she pedaled to the store, where she bought Theo a bag of gummy worms, the deluxe kind dusted with sugar. Back outside, the sky was heavy with gathering clouds. The poncho stuck to her skin. She was thirsty, but (as you know) she had no water bottle. *Women Spacefarers* hung like a rock between her shoulders. Why hadn't she gotten a book on goldfish care, or one with photos of kittens? (She'd read dozens already, but there can be no such thing as too many kitten books.)

Loah put on her helmet. Her pile of worries kept growing. Mama, Theo, Inspector Kipper, and she wasn't even going to think about the turret. *Pile* might not be the right word. *Mound. Hill. Great Pyramid.*

Not to mention. Not to mention the girl running away from home.

Home. For the first time in her life, Loah was not ready to go there. Not yet. Instead she turned her bike off the main road onto the smaller one that wound up and down and between green-gold fields. When the bike reached the fork in the road, it stopped.

Actually, it was Loah who stopped. Her hands squeezed the brakes, and her foot touched the ground, and her eyes (the obedient one and the wandering one together) gazed down the road that forked left. She imagined the girl standing at the foot of her driveway, quiet and watchful among the angry signs. Thumbs hooked under the straps of her bulging backpack, she peered patiently down the road, waiting for Loah to come back.

This was so silly! The girl—what was her name?—didn't expect Loah to return. She'd probably forgotten all about Loah. That thought might have made Loah turn around, but instead she told herself it gave her all the more reason to ride on and see for herself that the girl wasn't expecting her. Because once Loah knew that for sure, she could stop feeling bad, couldn't she? It would be a relief, wouldn't it? The sad, thin girl and her thieving little brother would be one less thing to fret about.

Loah pedaled down the road. Out here, the world had no lid. Unlike at home, there were almost no trees, only field and sky. Speaking of outer space—at night a person could probably see millions of stars out here. Maybe even a planet. Mars, the red planet; Saturn with its rings; or Jupiter and its many moons. At Loah's house, Earth's moon got snagged in tree branches, but here it would float straight up, like a helium balloon.

As she got closer to the bend, her heart rose as if *it* were a balloon. Around the curve, and there were the signs. You could almost hear them shouting.

KEEP OUT

Keep in, you weirdos

TRESPASSERS WILL BE PROSECUTED OR WORSE

The driveway was empty. Dust swirled in the gathering breeze.

Loah's body suddenly remembered how tired it was. Her legs filled with sand. Her head became a baked ham. She read and re-read the signs. The O in PROSECUTED was a jagged, empty hole. Loah waited a long time, just in case. To be sure. Beyond a doubt.

The breeze stiffened. It rippled and ruffled the meadow grass. Miss Rinker was right—it was going to rain. Loah slowly turned her bike around, just as a fluffy cloud with four legs sprang out of the tall grass and into the road. Its nose was the color of bubble gum. A wildflower dangled from its mouth.

"Baa!" It bounded toward her.

Loah dropped her bike. She threw out her arms and to her own amazement, the little creature ran straight to her. It was a goat, she realized, even more amazed. She circled it with her arms as the meadow grass parted again and out stumbled the girl. Who froze, equally amazed.

An amazement of girls.

"You came back," she said. "I knew you would."

"You did?" Loah rocked on her heels, and the baby goat took the chance to plant its hooves on her chest, do a reverse somersault, and escape back into the meadow.

"Aquaman!" cried the girl—or at least it sounded as if that was what she said. She raced after it.

Baby goats are nimble. Loah could almost hear it giggling as it pogo-sticked over rocks and thistle thickets. Its ears flew out like velvet wings as the two girls chased it. By the time Loah wrapped her arms around it again, she was a mess of sweat and scratches. When she collapsed in the sweet-smelling grass, it grinned at her from her arms. Its nose was shaped like a heart. If she'd ever seen anything more adorable, she couldn't remember.

The girl sank down next to Loah.

"It's . . . so . . . bouncy!" Loah gasped. "And so fluffy!"

"That's Angoras for you."

The goat was trying to squirm free, but the girl leaned over and knuckled its head till it surrendered and abruptly fell asleep in Loah's lap. Loah remembered how she'd tamed Bully. An animal wizard, that's what she was.

"All goats are escape artists," the girl said, "but Aquaman should really be named Houdini. He gets out of the pen all the time."

"Aquaman?"

"We're not supposed to name them." She appeared to be wearing the very same clothes as last time. "We milk the goats, shear them, and breed them. Some of them get butchered. My grandfather calls them our means of production."

Butchered? Loah felt woozy.

"Zeke names them, though. Usually after superheroes." She rolled her eyes.

"Zeke's your little brother?"

"Yup. I'm sorry he stole your water bottle."

A purple butterfly floated down to land on Loah's knee. Its wings opened and closed like the covers of a magical book. She stroked Aquaman's knobby little head. They wouldn't butcher *him*, would they?

"He's cute now," said the girl, wrinkling her nose. "But wait. Billy goats pee on themselves to attract the nannies."

"*What?*"

"You never smelled a worse stink in your entire life."

"Birds have strange mating rituals, too. The greater roadrunner dances around with a dead lizard to attract the female."

The girl laughed. Loah didn't often make people laugh, at least not in a nice way, and this girl's laugh was very nice. Like an underground stream bubbling up. She leaned back on her hands and looked at Loah the way she had the first time they met—expectantly, as if Loah had a secret talent. A trick up her sleeve. The breeze blew across Loah's sweaty arms and she shivered.

"What's your name?"

"Loah Londonderry. What's yours?"

The girl hesitated. Her fingers were long and thin, like twigs with the bark peeled off. Her face, which Loah had thought was tan, was actually covered in freckles. Hundreds. Maybe thousands. The butterfly lifted into the sky, and the girl watched it go before answering.

"Ellis Smith."

"That's nice. Ellis is . . . sophisticated."

"I like Loah, too. It's different, like you." Ellis's big toe, poking out of her sneaker, wiggled. "Different in a good way, I mean."

Loah smiled. The grass made a sort of nest around them.

"Did you just move here?" she asked. "I never saw you at school."

"I was born in the hollow." Ellis jutted her chin toward the hidden side of the hill. "I mean, literally. In the parlor. We don't go to school. We're self-educated." Her lips pressed together in a thin line. "We're self-everything. My grandfather doesn't trust institutions."

"Is that who you live with?"

"And my mother and Zeke. My grandmother died, and let's not even talk about my father."

Loah wanted to ask if it was her grandfather who'd been hollering at a squirrel the other day. She wanted to ask if Ellis had been planning to run away. Most of all, she wanted to ask how Ellis had known she'd come back here. But Ellis directed her dark eyes to a spot in the distance. *Enough questions,* said her expression.

The breeze made the meadow grass do the hula. The gray clouds bunched together into one rumbly mass. Loah had a long ride home, yet still she sat there, stroking Aquaman's curly coat. Often when she was with other people, Loah felt more lonesome than when she was alone. This didn't make sense, but she couldn't help it. Being with Ellis was different. Different in a good way.

Ellis's eyebrows knitted together. She pinched her bare leg.

"Tick," she said, holding it up with pincer-fingers.

It was pinhead-sized, but Loah saw a drop of blood on it. She gasped. Ellis looked puzzled.

"It's off. Don't worry."

"I know. I mean . . . Blood makes me woozy."

"Wuss," said Ellis, then immediately looked sorry.

"It's okay. I *am* a wuss about a lot of stuff."

Ellis squinched the bug between her fingers and tossed it away. Thunder rolled in the distance. Aquaman woke up and bleated a *baaa* that said he, at least, knew an open meadow was nowhere to be during an electrical storm. On the other side of the hill, out of sight, Bully began to bark.

"I better go." Loah reluctantly stood up. Aquaman bleated again, but she hated to put him down.

"Crew?" Ellis stood up, too. "What crew are you on?"

It took Loah a second to understand Ellis was reading the back of the poncho.

"Miss Rinker can't resist bargains."

"Miss Rinker?"

"She takes care of me. She and her brother, Theo."

"Are you an orphan?"

"No! Well, half." To her surprise, Loah's voice caught. On the other side of the hill, Bully stopped barking as abruptly as if he'd fallen over dead. By now the sky was the color of iron. "I have a mother, but she's away." Loah's voice quivered. "I haven't seen her in sixty-four days."

Ellis considered this. She was not a hasty person. She reminded Loah of Theo, except that she was a girl and he was an old man, and she had a deep-down restlessness the opposite of his deep-down contentedness.

"When's she coming back?" she asked.

"I don't know."

"Why?"

"Why don't I know? Or why is she gone so long?"

"Both."

"She went on an expedition in the Arctic tundra and . . . things got complicated."

"The Arctic!" Ellis's eyes grew wide. Her big toe wiggled. "Isn't that kind of dangerous?"

It was Loah's turn not to answer right away, and in the meantime the rain began. It was the kind of rain that sees no point in fooling around. All business, it bucketed down. Taking Aquaman from Loah's arms, Ellis had to raise her voice over the sudden gush and rush.

"Angoras can't take rain. I have to help get them all in the barn. Sorry you can't come, but you can't. I hope that poncho works."

Loah climbed on her bike. The rain was coming down so hard she could barely see two feet ahead. This was exactly the kind of weather that convinced a homebody never to leave home again.

As she pushed off, Ellis, still holding Aquaman, followed for a few steps.

"Where do you live? Is it far?"

"On the edge of town. The house with the turret."

"Oh." Ellis stopped in her tracks. "That place."

Loah flapped a goodbye and turned her bike toward home. The poncho fought to keep her dry, but the rain slapped her face and soaked her sneakers. The uneven country road filled with puddles, and the ditch alongside overflowed with muddy water.

I'd be better off with a boat, she thought, which made her think of Ferdinand Magellan sailing the unknown seas. When he found a new ocean, he named it Pacific, meaning peaceful and serene. Poor Magellan. Little did he know he was on his way to an agonizing death.

Today, the ride back was much longer than the ride there. At last the gleaming slates of the turret roof came into view. The car was gone, which Loah took as a good sign. Theo must be feeling better, just as Miss Rinker had predicted. Though Loah wished he hadn't gone out in this awful storm.

She put her bike in the garage, then stood in its doorway, preparing to make a dash through the rain to the house. Thunder boomed. Lightning forked.

Up in the turret windows, she saw a flash of red. Red the color of raw meat.

CHAPTER TWELVE

Don't be silly, she told herself as she huddled in the garage doorway. It was . . . it was a reflection of the branches waving in the wind.

Branches are not red, herself argued back.

Lightning then. My bad eye playing a trick.

Your eye does not play tricks.

If you've ever argued with yourself, you know how confusing it can be.

She pulled up the hood of her poncho, ran across the yard, up the back steps (careful on the rotten bottom one), and into the kitchen. The radio was tuned to the afternoon opera.

"Miss Rinker? I'm back."

She hung up her backpack and dripping poncho. The opera singers were engaged in a tortured duet. One of them was obviously going to die any minute. Loah went to the kitchen doorway and called again, louder this time.

"Miss Rinker?"

Had she gone with Theo? But why would Miss Rinker leave the radio on? She never wasted electricity. Theo's wild-ponies blanket lay in a heap on the floor. Loah folded it up, but instead of putting it on his chair, she held it close. In its bowl, her fish floated slant-wise, as if trying to lie down. Oh no! But when Loah leaned to look, it flicked its translucent golden tail. Still alive.

"Good fish," she said. "Where is everyone?"

Fish are condemned to silence. Imagine how painful that must be.

The only sounds were the rain on the roof and the doomed opera singers. Because of the trees, the house was always dim in summer, but this afternoon it was so murky Loah had to switch on the lights. When she did, she was startled to see bright red drops on the black-and-white tiles. The same red as that flash in the turret window. Woozy, she leaned against the table.

Where she saw the note, written on the back of a Bargain Blaster receipt. The printing was minuscule, wasting not an inch of paper or drop of ink.

Loah,
No help for it this time. Will call. Do not use stove or knives.
Miss R.

Loah clutched Theo's blanket. What could Miss Rinker mean? Had Theo gotten sicker? Had he fallen again? Could those red drops on the floor be what they looked like, no please no? Miss Rinker's driving was scary enough on a clear, calm day. But in this storm! Loah read the note again and saw how Miss Rinker's normally firm handwriting wobbled. Had she been . . . afraid?

Of the many things Miss Rinker scorned, fear topped the list. Thunderstorms, centipedes, clowns, garden snakes, sirens, basements, mean teachers, and midnight intruders didn't bother her, and over the years she'd soothed Loah's fears on all these things and many more.

If Miss Rinker was afraid, it was serious.

One of the opera singers gave a piercing scream. Loah snapped the radio off.

She tried to think. Had they gone to a doctor? But which one? Certainly not her pediatrician, the only doctor she knew. The hospital maybe. There was one on the far side of town. She could call there and ask.

But Loah hated talking on the phone, especially to strangers and most especially to strangers who might tell her bad news. She stared out the window. A beetle landed, clung to the screen for a desperate moment, and was blown away.

She should never have left them. She should have disobeyed Miss Rinker and stayed home. Staying home was always the best course of action! This proved it. She would have been here to help. She'd be with them now, wherever they were. Instead she was alone, with no idea what to do.

Thunder clapped the house between iron hands.

Loah curled up in Theo's E-Z Boy and pulled his wild-ponies blanket over her head. She tucked her knees under her chin and hugged them close.

Inside an egg, it is always peaceful. The baby bird is never lonesome, never scared or confused. Outside, the wind can howl and the rain lash, but inside its shell, the chick has nothing to worry about. Tucked deep in the nest, it hears its parent's heart beat out the message, *Fear not. While I have you beneath my wing, nothing will ever hurt you.*

The phone rang. Loah tossed the blanket aside.

"Hello?"

"Loah?" Miss Rinker's voice was as faint as if she were calling from another galaxy.

"Miss Rinker!"

For a long moment, the two of them just breathed. In out, in out.

"I'm at the hospital. My brother had another fall," Miss Rinker whispered as if revealing a shameful secret. "I did what I could, but . . . it seems he needed stitches."

Relief surged through Loah. Stitches were terrible, but not life-threatening.

"Then he'll be all right. You'll be home soon."

A pause.

"He's not coming home. I demanded an explanation, and they said, Why don't you sit down and have a nice cup of tea. *Tea!* Do they think *I'm* sick? I drink coffee and I drink it black. Do you know what one doctor called me?"

"What?"

"*Dear!* Calm yourself, *dear*, she said. As if I were a blubbering child."

Loah pictured Miss Rinker in a hospital corridor, wearing her cactus sweater and goose-feather hat. When she was upset, Miss Rinker had a habit of pounding her fist on whatever was in the vicinity. Loah prayed it wouldn't be a nurse or doctor. She tried to think of something soothing to say.

"I'm sure it will be all right. Theo will rest, and then—"

"His heart leaks."

What could she mean? Theo had the most dependable, sturdy heart of anyone Loah knew.

"From the scarlet fever he had in the orphanage." Miss Rinker made a sound like a plugged-up drain. *Glup.* "I remember it like it was yesterday. They took him to the infirmary, and I was forbidden to visit. He was only four years old. He cried and held out his little arms to me as they took him away."

Loah picked up Theo's blanket again. She wrapped it around herself.

"I marched into that infirmary, and when they tried to throw me out I bit them. More than once, I'm proud to say. I had all my own teeth then. You'd better believe they let me stay."

"Please don't bite anyone, Miss Rinker."

"You hate thunderstorms. You'll need your supper. I'll be home as soon as I can."

"You can't leave Theo all alone." Loah saw him in a glacial white hospital bed, attached to beeping machines, snaking wires, evil tubes. Strangers came and went, and nothing, nothing whatsoever was familiar. Theo was a homebody, just like her. The hospital would be his worst nightmare. "You have to stay."

"But . . ." Miss Rinker's voice faltered. "What about you? Even I can't be in two places at once."

Thinking of Theo in the hospital was painful enough. Thinking of him there all alone was unbearable.

"Don't leave him, Miss Rinker. You've always been by his side. He needs you."

"Do not tell me what . . ." Miss Rinker's voice trailed off in confusion.

"I'll be all right," Loah said. "I can take care of myself till you get back. Miss Rinker?"

Miss Rinker was speaking to someone else. "Who else would I be?" she demanded. "Who are *you* is the question?"

Loah waited, watching the wind thrash the tree branches. Imagine being a wild creature fending for yourself against that wind and wet. The birds had to. Thank goodness she had a house. Thank goodness her natural habitat was safe and dry and not wild. Thank goodness—

Miss Rinker was back. "The doctors have all ganged up and want to talk to me."

"Do whatever they say, okay?"

"Make yourself a sandwich for supper. Do not touch the stove! Do your ocular exercises and watch that silly show of yours, *Lonely Family*—"

"*One and Only Family.*"

"Loah Londonderry!" Miss Rinker suddenly sounded as if she was being torn in half. Coming apart at the seams. "Are you sure you can manage till I get home? It could be very late."

Loah leaned against the table. She was not sure. Not sure at all. In its bowl, her fish blew a stream of silvery bubbles and flicked its tail. It swam close to the glass as if trying to send her a silent, fishy message.

"Miss Rinker, I'm not alone. I have my pet fish, remember? Thanks to you and Theo. It will keep me company." She could hear another voice, low and urgent, in the background. "Talk to the doctors. Don't worry about me. And please—please give Theo my love. Tell him I bought him a surprise."

"I'll be home as soon as I can."

Loah set down the phone. She looked around the empty kitchen.

Up till this moment in her life, she'd always assumed that empty was empty. Now she understood: There were degrees. There was such a thing as *very* empty.

Carefully, she folded Theo's blanket and set it on his lounger. She wet a paper towel, squinched her eyes, and scrubbed the red splotches off the floor. Upstairs, she changed out of her damp shorts and T-shirt, which smelled like grass and baby goat. She climbed the steps to the attic, where the doors to Theo's and Miss Rinker's rooms stood open. They were neat and sparse, what Loah imagined rooms in an orphanage would look like. At the sight of the empty beds, her heart faltered. She set out buckets to catch the leaks, then went back downstairs to close windows and mop wet sills. In the library, she sank into the chair at her mother's desk where, in the midst of the feathery, papery, eggshell-y mess, the phone sat silent.

Very silent.

Are you an orphan?

When is she coming back?

Isn't that dangerous?

The phone rang. Loah grabbed it.

"Hello?"

An earnest man offered to waterproof her basement (which did, in fact, need it). He could beat anyone else's price and was prepared to offer a money-back, once-in-a-lifetime guarantee. When Loah didn't reply, he took it as encouragement. He spoke reassuringly about trenches and hydraulic cement. Any basement, the man promised, could be made shipshape-tight. Even basements that flooded badly could be saved and restored.

Who knew a stranger could be so comforting? When, at last, he gave up and said goodbye, Loah missed him.

Her stomach growled, reminding her she hadn't eaten since breakfast, but when she went to the kitchen to make a sandwich, she discovered they were out of bread. Rummaging in the cupboard, she found a can of pea soup. Miss Rinker couldn't see her, but Loah, who always found comfort in being obedient, didn't turn on the stove. She ate the congealed soup cold from the can, then locked the doors, fetched the fishbowl from the kitchen, and switched off the stag-head chandelier. Slowly (remember how tired she already was, and that she'd ridden her bike through a storm, and that *athletic* was the last word to describe her), she climbed the stairs to her room, where she set her fish on her bedside table next to the photo of her and Mama. She did her ocular exercises, climbed into bed, and watched *One and Only Family* on her laptop. Loah waited for the show to make her feel content and drowsy, as if she'd eaten a dozen sugar cookies. Instead, the longer she watched, the more forlorn she felt, as if she had her nose pressed to a bakery window full of treats she'd never be allowed to taste.

Outside, something large crashed to the ground. Down the end of the hall, from behind the turret door, came an echoing thunk.

Loah pulled the covers up. The wind blew. The walls creaked. The windows rattled. As the hours went by and Miss Rinker did not return, she grew more and more anxious. Though her window was shut, she heard, undaunted by the storm, the shivery call of a screech owl. This bird is only nine inches tall, with sweet little tufts that almost look like ears. If you saw it in the light of day, it might remind you of a kitten. Yet few things are more blood-chilling than its long, tremulous wail. If you've ever watched a horror movie, or gone to a Halloween haunted house, you'd recognize that ghostly sound.

A lullaby, her mother called it.

Every night of her life, Loah had slept with Rinkers overhead. They'd watched over her like beaky, scraggy storks.

Tonight she lay in bed, covers to her chin, with no one between her and the endless dark sky.

CHAPTER THIRTEEN

Here is how many birds sleep: They find a nice thicket, a cozy hole in a tree, or a branch where they can snuggle close to a trunk still warm from the sun. They fluff their feathers, tuck their beaks, pull one leg up to their soft bellies, and *good night.*

No one knows for sure if they dream.

Just before dawn, they wake. And here is another thing that no one, even devoted ornithologists like Dr. Londonderry, understands for sure: why they immediately begin to sing as if their lives depend on it.

Are they so thrilled it's a new day? Are they letting their friends (and enemies) know they've survived another long, perilous night? Scientists agree that birdsong is one of the most complex and glorious phenomena in all of nature. Yet how birds acquire it, and why, and what this remarkable skill might reveal about communication in general—much of this remains uncertain.

The bird brain holds many mysteries.

When Loah opened her eyes the next morning, sunlight streamed through her tall, cracked windows. She lay still, straining her ears for sounds of life inside the house, but all she heard was the familiar sighs and murmurs of the old house itself.

Maybe you've had the experience of suspecting, in a dark corner of your brain, something you really, truly wish wasn't so. Maybe you've done what Loah did now, which was to put off discovering the truth as long as possible, as if that might somehow change the truth, which is of course impossible.

The human brain holds many mysteries, too.

Slowly she climbed out of bed. She pushed open her windows and let the morning birdsong pour in. The ground was soft from the rain, and the worm-eaters bustled about. An American robin cocked its head, listened to the ground, then *zap*—the poor worm was a goner.

Loah tried to brush her hair, which bristled with seeds and pods from chasing Aquaman through the meadow. Happily, her fish, like the birds, had survived another night. It even looked a little frisky. She performed her ocular exercises, and then, having run out of ways to stall, she carefully carried the fishbowl down to the kitchen, where, just as she had feared, the two E-Z Boys stood empty. Very.

The phone rang. Miss Rinker, she thought, and dived to pick it up. When she saw the number displayed, her heart cartwheeled.

"Mama!"

"Sweetie! My sweet sweet sweetie!"

Never, ever had Loah been happier to hear her mother's voice, and that was saying something. "I've been waiting and waiting for you to call. Where are you?"

"Approximately five kilometers northwest of Kunaat." Dr. Londonderry gave the GPS coordinates, which Loah memorized. "I'm so sorry to be out of touch. The weather is a catastrophe. Windy, cloudy, and horribly, unnaturally warm. My jeep got stuck in mud! If a couple of kindly hunters hadn't come by, I'm not sure—"

"But you're all right?"

"I've hit some unexpected rough patches, and I'm a bit low on rations, and keeping this phone charged is nearly impossible with the cloud cover. But that's all in a day's work. The land, though! The terrain this far west is worse than I knew. The satellite images can't begin to tell the full story. Yesterday I saw a herd of musk oxen that were nothing but skin and bones." Her mother's voice caught. "They broke my heart. For a moment, I lost hope."

Loah's own heart twisted. Musk oxen were adorable, shaggy creatures with long, mournful faces. Huge as they were, they lived on moss, lichen, and Arctic flowers.

"But then," said Mama. "Then! Oh sweetie—my hunch was right. She's come to the coast to nest."

Loah fell into her mother's chair. "You saw her?"

"I heard her call again—unfortunately, it was too windy to record. But with the binocs I caught another unmistakable glimpse of her in flight. What an amazing girl she is—fooled us all! Hundreds of other species driven into extinction, over a quarter of existing species *threatened* with extinction—but our girl! She's survived! And she did it quietly, without any of us scientists ever noticing."

Loah leaned back as her mother launched into a description of the loah bird's habits. Loah the human had heard it all before—how the bird lived on insects and seeds, how it migrated in winter but returned to the tundra to breed, how the female, with the patch of gold on her wings, was more colorful than the male, which was unusual. She could have recited it all by heart, but she was so befuddled, and her mother so excited, that she didn't interrupt. The loah bird, her mother went on, laid her eggs on the rocky shore. The fate of those two or three eggs was always dicey but never more so than now, what with the violent, unpredictable storms, the rising seas, the competition for dwindling food supplies, and the increase in predators.

"The red fox has migrated here for the first time—did I tell you that, sweetie? The temperature has risen enough for it to live here and now it will compete with the Arctic fox for..." Her mother paused. "Loah? Are you there?"

"Yes, Mama."

"The bad news is, I haven't seen any sign of the male. I'm hoping to spy him when I make it to the coast. Normally she incubates, while he's the food source for her and the chicks.... I really hope nothing's happened to him."

In the silence Loah heard the gusting wind.

"Mama..."

"You understand how crucial it is for me to stay, don't you? To find our loah and, if there really are eggs, to protect them till they hatch. It's all too possible these are the last ones! Think what a tremendous loss that would be. Our bird, but so much more as well. The ties between living organisms are so intricate and dependent— pull one tiny thread of the tapestry, and the whole thing can unravel. If I actually document a sighting, I could get funding to do the work I've always... Oh sweetie! I'm sorry. The last thing you need is a lecture. And my battery is running low again. Tell me quick-quick: How are you? Fine, right? No school! Home every day, the way you like. Knitting, reading, everything quiet and lovely..."

"The thing is—Theo had a fall. He needed stitches."

"What?" Her mother gasped. "Oh no! Miss Rinker actually went to a doctor? Put her on, sweetie. Hurry, before my phone dies."

"But she's—" *Gone.* The word was nearly out before Loah swallowed it back.

"What? Miss Rinker's what?"

"Miss Rinker, she's..." Loah flattened her palm on the tabletop. "She's Miss Rinker."

"Ha." Her mother's laugh was uncertain. "I suppose that's true, no matter what. She's probably mercilessly scolding Theo while taking tender care of him."

"Probably."

Should she tell her mother about Theo's heart? About being left here alone? Yes she should. No she shouldn't. Mama would get so upset, she'd probably decide to come home, and what was the good in that? It would take her at least two days to get here, and by then, for sure, Theo and Miss Rinker would be back. Meanwhile, her mother—the planet, really—would lose the chance, possibly the last chance ever, to find and save the loah.

"Loah?"

She pictured a tiny egg lying on the rough, rocky shore. Its mother tried to protect it, but the waves crashed. The wind howled. Predators crept close. Inside, the baby bird had no idea of the danger it was in, no idea how scary the world outside was. Loah's heart tilted. How could she ask Mama to abandon the egg and its mother?

"I miss you so much," Mama was saying. "You're the first thing I think of every morning and the last thing—"

A hollow, hungry howl made Loah catch her breath. "What was that? It sounds like a wolf pack!"

"Just another bit of nasty weather. I need . . . batten the hatches. Tell . . . Rinkers . . ."

"Wait. Don't hang up yet."

That wind sounded fierce as any predator. It had risen so suddenly. And what had Mama said about being low on rations? And she was all alone. Fear beat up inside Loah. She was making a bad mistake. She should convince her mother to come home, right now. Home, where all was safe.

"Mama, listen. I need to tell you—"

"Loah, sweetie, I love . . ."

And she was gone.

Again.

Upstairs in her room, Loah looked at the picture over her bed. The loah was so small, so plain. So *homely*. Her only bit of beauty was the gold on her wings, a patch so small you'd miss it if you didn't look closely. Leaning closer to the picture, Loah felt the back of her throat close up.

"I need her, too, you know," she whispered.

CHAPTER FOURTEEN

Theodore Rinker is in ICU and unable to accept calls," said the hospital information person. "Would you like to be connected to the nurses' station?"

"No thank you," Loah whispered, and hung up.

I see you? She hoped that meant they were keeping a close eye on Theo.

It had taken Loah forever to work up the nerve to call, and now she didn't know what to do. Miss Rinker's words sounded in her head: In times of worry, the best thing to do is keep busy. (Miss Rinker believed the same thing was true in times of joy. In fact, at all times in life.) Loah tied on Miss Rinker's THIS IS WHAT FABULOUS LOOKS LIKE! apron. She scrubbed out yesterday's oatmeal pot. (Was it really only yesterday?) She fed the fish and checked that its water was clean. She fetched the mending basket and sewed a button onto Theo's shirt. It smelled like Theo—soap and salt. It had a gummy worm in the pocket. She carefully picked the lint off it, then ate it in tiny bites as she knitted and purled several more rows on the scarf she was making for Mama. Then, seeing she'd dropped stitches, she pulled the rows out and did them over again.

Still no Miss Rinker.

She found a pair of scissors and a ball of twine, tucked them into the pockets of the apron along with both her cell phone and the kitchen landline receiver, and went outside. She started to gather up the twigs and branches the storm had scattered everywhere. Think how surprised and pleased Miss Rinker would be to come home and find the fallen branches tidied into neat bundles.

Something resembling a meteorite lay in the driveway.

A chunk of turret was what it was. That must have been the crash she'd heard last night. It had come loose in the storm and fallen to the ground, where it lay like a giant rotten tooth.

The house was falling to pieces! Her habitat wasn't just threatened—it was endangered.

Loah, who rarely got angry, felt the flush of what was, definitely, anger.

She marched to the garage and got the wheelbarrow. Hoisting the masonry required strength, which (like courage) she had in only limited supply. But she couldn't leave it there. A crumbling turret would get a checkmark on Inspector Kipper's list for sure. Loah pushed the wheelbarrow behind the garage and dumped it out, hoping that, if the inspector came back, he wouldn't find it. Stepping out into the yard, she'd just caught her breath when something snatched it away all over again.

An enormous bird was perched on the roof. Its beak was hooked, its neck wrinkled, its head bald. When the bird spread its dark wings, they were as wide as Loah was tall.

Turkey vulture, aka buzzard. She'd never seen a real one but recognized it from her mother's books. Unlike most birds, turkey vultures have a highly developed sense of smell, enabling them to find dead things. Which is what they thrive on. Their heads are featherless, the better to burrow into bloody, messy carcasses and pick the bones clean.

A volt. A group of vultures is a volt. (Who gets to make up these names, anyway? Don't you wish it was you?)

Thank goodness there was no volt on Loah's roof. One vulture was more than enough, thank you.

As she watched, the bird folded its wings like a villain pulling his cape close around him. It shifted from foot to foot and uttered a sound somewhere between a groan and a grunt.

"What are you doing here? You've made a mistake. There's nothing dead here." She flapped Miss Rinker's apron. "Get! Be on your way!"

If you've ever tried to look a bird in the eye, you know it's practically impossible. Yet this vulture locked eyes with her and didn't blink.

Even with humans, Loah was terrible at staring contests. With a vulture she had zero hope. Dropping her bundle of sticks, she hurried back inside. Where, at last, the landline rang. She fumbled it from the apron pocket.

"Hello? Hello?"

"Theo had an event," said Miss Rinker.

This seemed good news. Loah imagined a birthday party or wedding reception. Though who'd hold an event at a hospital?

A cone of silence descended.

"Miss Rinker? Did you attend the event, too?"

"In plain English, his heart stopped."

Loah's did, too.

"A machine got it going again," Miss Rinker said. "He's in ICU—the intensive care unit."

This was why she hadn't come home! Loah's thoughts spun to the vulture. Many cultures believe birds have the power to foretell events. Vultures, she was pretty sure, were not good omens.

"Is he all right? How could that happen?"

"The doctors say the scarlet fever scarred his valves." Miss Rinker sounded as if she were reciting from a text. "They're narrowed and leaky and . . ." All at once she interrupted herself. "Just think if we'd stayed home instead of coming here!" She sounded furious. "The doctors say we'd have lost him."

"No!"

"We'd have lost him!" Miss Rinker repeated, enraged. Who was she angry at? "He wouldn't have survived!" She ranted and fumed some more until, like an engine sputtering out of fuel, at last she whispered, "It's my fault."

Loah had never seen Miss Rinker cry, and she was glad she couldn't see her now, because just listening was terrible enough.

"He's always been frail." Miss Rinker gulped, and when she spoke again, her voice was small as a child's. "I knew he was getting weaker. I was afraid something was wrong. But I've always taken care of him. I thought I still could."

"Miss Rinker, you *have* taken care of him! Very, very good care. It's not your fault."

Miss Rinker wept.

Ever since she was younger than Loah, Miss Rinker had taken care of other people. First her brother. Now Loah. When Dr. Londonderry was home, Miss Rinker looked after her, too. Who'd ever taken care of Miss Rinker? No one, Loah realized with a shock of sorrow. Miss Rinker's mother had abandoned her. Nearly all her life, she'd had nobody to watch over her, to help and comfort and protect her.

"Miss Rinker, why don't you sit down? I know you hate tea, but you need to keep hydrated. Have you eaten? Maybe they have saltines in the vending machines."

"They want to put him under the knife," said Miss Rinker.

"The knife!"

"Open-heart surgery."

Woozy, Loah leaned against the wall.

"Are...are the doctors sure?" she asked. "Couldn't they just give him some medicine?"

"They said I could get a second opinion, but they are nothing if not sure." Accustomed to being in charge, Miss Rinker sounded emptied out, like a dried-up seedpod rattling in the wind. She blew her nose. She cleared her throat. "I hope you don't think I was crying just now."

Outside the kitchen window, a ruby-throated hummingbird hovered at Theo's feeder. A hummingbird beats its wings eighty times per second, which is such hard work, its heart has to be enormous, compared to its body.

Theo's heart was a hummingbird heart.

After she and Miss Rinker said goodbye, Loah set the phone down gently, as if it were alive and she might injure it. Everything felt breakable. The phone, the table, even the air.

CHAPTER FIFTEEN

When Loah was small, her mother told her bedtime stories about the snow goose, which lines its nest with down plucked from its own breast, and the emperor penguin, which doesn't eat anything for the entire two months it cradles its egg atop its faithful feet. She told Loah about birds that migrated for thousands of miles and birds that lived their whole lives in sight of the tree where they hatched. (You can guess which Loah would have been.)

Sometimes Loah asked for a story about a princess or a cat instead. But Mama was such a good storyteller—her voice round and warm, the words tumbling over one another in her eagerness—that every story was wonderful. Loah's eyes would grow heavy, but she'd fight to stay awake till the end.

There was one story they both loved best of all. Old as Loah was now, Mama would still snuggle down beside her and tell it.

"You were due in two weeks, and I still didn't know what to name you. Your father died before we'd decided, and I guess I was waiting for some kind of sign. Maybe from him? Maybe from the universe? We'd only just moved into this house when he died. I hadn't realized how big the place was. How very, very empty it could feel. I was so sad and lonely. My heart was lost and I couldn't find it."

Mama would pause, and Loah would lay her head on Mama's chest. She'd feel the steady beat of Mama's heart, and couldn't imagine it ever being lost.

"It was a chilly, gray, ugly day. I'd canceled my classes at the university, and I was trying to find the energy to make some tea when you . . . What did you do, Loah? Do you remember?"

Loah would smile. "Of course not!"

"I do. I was used to feeling you move, but this was different. It wasn't a roll or a poke or a kick. It was more of a . . . a hug. An inside-of-me hug. How did you do that?" She'd wind one of Loah's curls around her finger. "That hug made me feel so much better. I got my tea and went to my desk, determined to do some work. No sooner did I open my computer than I read about the first sighting of a loah in over thirty years. It was unofficial and blah blah blah, but my heart—my heart didn't care."

Snuggled close, Loah would feel that heart beat faster.

"I studied the blurry photo, and I could see it on her wing: that unmistakable streak of gold, like a shining ray of hope. Like a promise that everything wasn't over, and the world was still a place brimming with surprise and wonder and beauty for the finding. I got so excited. And I guess you did, too, sweetie. You decided you couldn't wait a moment longer and had to hatch that very night."

When Loah looked up, Mama's eyes would be bright with tears.

"As soon as I saw you, I knew your name."

By the time Miss Rinker came home from the hospital, it was late. Purple circles ringed her eyes, and her shoulders were bent like old clothes hangers. She allowed Loah to unlace and pull her shoes off, which was a little terrifying, since Miss Rinker's feet resembled root vegetables, and since she'd never before admitted she needed help. When Loah fetched her slippers, Miss Rinker stared as if she had no idea what they were. Loah slid them onto her feet.

"Just rest. I'll make our supper," Loah said.

"Don't be ridiculous," said Miss Rinker. But she didn't stir from her E-Z Boy.

Loah mashed overripe bananas. She arranged the rest of the liverwurst on a plate and spooned pickled beets into a bowl. She set the table with silverware, dishes, and HAPPY NEW YEAR! napkins from Bargain Blaster, and together they ate.

Afterward, they climbed to the second floor. At the foot of the rickety attic steps, Loah kept watch as Miss Rinker, hand gripping the railing, slippers shuffling, climbed up, growing smaller before Loah's very eyes.

When she turned, her eyes fell on the turret door at the end of the corridor.

Dr. Londonderry wasn't here. Neither was Theo, and Miss Rinker was a shadow of her former self. If Loah didn't take care of things, who would?

Drawing a breath, she forced herself to walk the length of the corridor and test the turret door. Shut tight, just as she'd left it. Yet she stood there a moment, listening.

Something listened back.

CHAPTER SIXTEEN

Loah wanted to see Theo, but the hospital scared her. Other than being born, she'd never been inside one. She wasn't the kind of child to break a leg or stuff a marble up her nose. She'd seen enough shows, though, to know that there'd be doctors rushing bloody patients down the corridors, PA systems blaring *Code Blue!*, people weeping in waiting rooms. Loah might get so upset she'd start to cry. When she cried, Theo got so upset they wound up having to comfort each other, and that surely was not what Theo needed now.

In the morning she helped Miss Rinker put on her shoes, then hunted for the car keys, which had vanished. She finally found them in Miss Rinker's dresser drawer. (Miss Rinker's underwear was a sight Loah had never expected to see and hoped never to see again.) Hat on her head, Miss Rinker paused by the door.

"You might go shopping. Last night's dinner was a bit . . . spare." She coughed. Her caterpillar eyebrows gave a startling twitch. "Go to the store and buy something you'd like. A frozen pizza, maybe."

Miss Rinker might as well have suggested Loah buy herself a pony. Alarm bells clanged. Was there something she wasn't telling

Loah? Was Theo even worse than she'd let on? Goose feather quivering, Miss Rinker hurried out the door.

Loah researched open-heart surgery. Or tried to. No sooner did she get to the phrase "chest incision" than she became too woozy to read any further and had to shut her laptop.

She took money from the sugar jar (you didn't think they had sugar in there, did you?) and though the sun shone, not a cloud in sight, she put on her poncho. This was silly, as babyish as keeping a baby blanket under her pillow, but the poncho made her feel more secure. As if Miss Rinker and Theo were with her, watching over her.

Outside, she plucked fallen leaves and twigs from the birdbaths, topped off the feeders, and filled the hummingbird feeder with nectar. Then she rode her bike to the store, where she bought two frozen pizzas and set them in her basket. She was determined to pedal straight home before they could defrost, but no sooner did she climb back on her bike than her head swam with pictures of Ellis. Her many freckles. Her expressive big toe. Her laugh like a little underground stream bubbling up. Ellis watching the purple butterfly lift into the sky. Ellis saying, *I knew you'd come back.*

Loah twisted her handlebars back and forth. Ellis was like a new star or an unmapped continent. Something wonderful that had always been there, waiting to be discovered.

Her front wheel had made a pattern in the dust, and Loah traced it with her shoe. She forced herself to remember what had happened last time when, instead of going straight home the way she was supposed to, instead of returning to Theo who was sick, she'd taken the side road.

Disaster. That's what.

Home. That's where she belonged.

Keeping her eyes straight ahead as best she could (the weak one kept tugging), she pedaled home.

Where the vulture lurked on the roof.

It spread its drab wings. It shifted its scaly feet. Loah, who was far from beautiful, tried never to judge others on appearances, but vultures were ugly. Hideous. It was hard to believe that even another vulture could love one.

"You are in the wrong place! Shoo!" She windmilled her arms. "Get out!" She flapped the poncho.

The other birds ignored it. As long as they were alive, they had nothing to fear. The dead—that's who vultures were interested in.

"There's nothing dead here. There never was and never will be, I promise! Find someplace else to haunt!"

The bird locked eyes with her. It was trying to tell her something, something Loah was sure she did not want to know.

She grabbed the frozen pizzas from her bike basket and scurried inside. Later, when she cautiously checked, the roof was vulture-free.

That night when Miss Rinker got home, Loah asked permission to turn on the stove and use a knife. She baked a pizza and whipped up instant mashed potatoes. She sliced a cucumber. Though she'd never cooked a thing in her life, it all turned out well, and she felt proud as she set the food on the table. Miss Rinker ate two helpings.

Loah fed her goldfish, who did several thank-you laps around its bowl. The fish grew peppier with every day. It was getting used to its new environment, maybe even feeling happy here. Loah sprinkled in more food. Who knew feeding others was so satisfying? She was already thinking about what she'd cook next when Miss Rinker folded her hands on the table.

"The surgery is scheduled for tomorrow."

"Tomorrow? You mean . . . tomorrow?"

Loah had been hoping the doctors would discover they'd made a mistake. Theo only needed rest, not surgery. A bowl of soup and a good, long nap and his heart would be just fine. His hummingbird heart.

The look on Miss Rinker's face told her how childish that hope had been.

"The surgery will take at least three hours but maybe more. It depends on whether there are . . . complications." Miss Rinker grabbed a BE MY VALENTINE napkin. "I'll have to go very early. I'll call you as soon as it's over."

"Over?"

"Not *over* over. I didn't mean . . ." Miss Rinker began to shred the napkin. "You know what I mean."

Because of the trees, night fell earlier here than in the rest of the world. By now, the kitchen windows were black rectangles. Loah could see their reflections wavering on the glass, while on the other side, the darkness tried to get in. Much as the hospital scared her, how could she let Miss Rinker go there all alone?

"I could come with you," she said. "I mean, I want to. We can wait together."

Miss Rinker looked up from her napkin shredding. A smile flitted across her face, but was gone as quickly as it came.

"A hospital is no place for someone who gets light-headed at the mere mention of blood," she said.

"If I start to feel woozy, I'll put my head between my knees," Loah promised.

Miss Rinker had reduced the napkin to smithereens. Shredded paper hearts littered the table. She seemed to hesitate, then looked away.

"I'd rather face this alone," she said quietly. "It's what I'm accustomed to."

Loah's eyes filled with tears. She didn't know if the tears were for Miss Rinker, Theo, herself, or all of them at once.

Miss Rinker lifted her sharp chin. She rapped the table with her knuckles, as if calling herself to attention.

"You'll stay home." She swept the torn hearts into a small pile. "It will be one less thing to worry about."

Loah was a *thing to worry about*. The words cut her to the quick.

Miss Rinker believed in speaking the truth, even if it hurt. Especially if it hurt. Now she crossed the room and dropped the paper shreds in the trash.

"I promised my brother you'd call him."

He didn't answer the phone, and when they tried again later, he sounded groggy and hoarse, as if he'd swum up from the bottom of the sea. Loah still ached from Miss Rinker's words, but she tried to push the hurt away and pay attention to Theo. She told him how well her fish was doing, and how she was keeping the birdbaths clean and the feeders full, and that as soon as she was allowed, she'd visit him. Lowering her voice, she told him she'd bring gummy worms. Soon, she told him, he would be better. Soon he would come home.

"Home," she repeated, and was sure she heard him smile.

CHAPTER SEVENTEEN

Once while she was playing Egg, Loah had a disturbing thought. How could a baby bird breathe in there? Where did it get air?

"A bird's egg is permeable," Dr. Londonderry had explained. "It has minuscule holes that let in air. Isn't it amazing? The shell is that thin, but at the same time it's strong enough to take the weight of the parent bird incubating it. Its oval shape and convex surface—they make it perfect for withstanding pressure." Not for nothing had Dr. Londonderry written *The Egg: Nature's Greatest Feat of Engineering*. She'd stroked Loah's curls and smiled the smile that turned her plain face beautiful. "As if that's not enough, eggs come in a myriad of sizes and colors. Some are plain as dirt, while others are exquisite jewels. But no matter what they look like, eggs all have the same job. In the end, they're meant to break."

The next morning, Loah woke just as the birds began to sing. She rushed downstairs, but she was too late. Miss Rinker was gone. A note written on a strip of cardboard torn from a saltine box was propped against the (not) sugar bowl.

Keep bus.

Miss R.

Busy, she meant. Standing in the (very) empty kitchen, Loah hated the word with all her heart. Keeping busy was for people who were not in charge. Keeping busy was a plot to prevent them from remembering that they were small, helpless things to worry about.

Loah kicked Miss Rinker's E-Z Boy. She opened a cupboard and slammed it shut. Then opened it again, took out a can of sardines, and threw it. Then picked it up. At last she hurled herself into Theo's lounger, pulled up his blanket, hugged her legs, and tucked her chin to her chest. Closing her eyes, she tried to imagine nature's most perfect construction curving around her, protecting her from every harm. Her mother bird nestled over her, tucking her close and snug.

Within minutes, Loah's legs cramped. Her neck kinked. It became hard to breathe. Back in the day when she'd played Egg often, the game had comforted her, but now it was painful. She shifted this way and that, trying to cozy herself into the shell, but it was useless. She no longer fit.

Who knew being safe could hurt?

A rap on the back door made her jump. Who could it be? A classmate on a dare? Inspector Kipper with his dastardly clipboard? She held her breath and scrunched herself smaller. Ouch. Her leg muscles twitched. Her arms grew numb. *Ouch.*

Another rap, louder this time.

Pretend not to hear. They'll give up and go away.

"Loah? Are you all right?"

Loah peeked from under the blanket to spy Ellis's freckled nose squished flat against the window screen. She jumped up and ran down the back steps (careful on the last one). Ellis wore the usual washed-out T-shirt, rolled-up jeans, and holey sneakers, but she'd added a faded denim jacket. Her bulging backpack leaned against the steps.

"Are you all right?" she repeated, worried. "You looked like you were sick."

Loah might have said the same words Ellis once said to her—*I knew you'd come*. But she hadn't known. Ellis coming here was the best kind of gift, one you didn't know you wanted, very much wanted, till someone gave it to you. Before Loah could say any of this, Zeke zoomed into the yard on a beater bike. His face was flushed, and his once-spiky green hair drooped. He skidded to a halt and toppled over sideways.

"What are you doing here?" cried Ellis.

Ignoring his sister, Zeke scrambled to his feet and advanced on Loah. "This is all your fault!" he said.

"Me?"

"She never ran away all the way before. Just to the bottom of the driveway. It's all 'cause of you, you fat, cockeyed, robot-alien birdbrain!"

"That's enough out of you," said Ellis, yanking him by the neck of his shirt. "Go sit down." She pointed at a lawn chair. "Now."

"You can't make—"

"You know I can, and you know I will."

Sulking and pouting, Zeke threw himself into the chair. Ellis turned to Loah.

"Sorry. I didn't know he was following me. Don't take his idiotic name-calling personally."

She gave her brother another poke. Perched in the ivy on the side of the house, a house finch launched into its jolly song. Ellis looked all around, and her narrow face slowly filled with wonder.

"When you said you lived in this house I was surprised. From the road it looks kind of deserted. It still kind of looks deserted, to tell you the truth. But enchanted-deserted."

A perfect description, in Loah's opinion.

"Are the Stinkers here?" Ellis asked.

"Rinkers!" Loah smiled in spite of herself. "No, they're not."

"Are you hungry?"

Loah realized she was. Starving.

Ellis opened her backpack and took out a sandwich wrapped in paper. It was made from thick slices of what looked and smelled like homemade bread. When Ellis held out half, Loah's mouth watered in a way that was embarrassing. But what was that in the middle? Loah never ate anything she hadn't eaten before.

"No thanks."

"It's almond butter," Ellis said. "Try it. It's good."

It was. Not just the almond butter but also the honey, oceans of honey, what Miss Rinker would consider a year's supply of honey. Loah tried to eat slowly but the sandwich was the most delicious thing she'd eaten in months. She licked her fingers, then licked them again. Sparrows clustered, hoping for crumbs, but she'd eaten every last bite.

Meanwhile Zeke escaped his lawn chair. He shinnied up a maple tree, hung from a branch, dropped to the ground. He gathered woody seedpods from the sweetgum and pelted their feet.

"Just ignore him," said Ellis. "He'll go away."

"No I won't. Not 'less you come with me," Zeke said.

"He pretends he's so tough," Ellis told Loah. "But he cries when he squishes a firefly by mistake."

"That was when I was little!"

"Like last week!"

"I hate you!"

"Not as much as I hate you." Ellis noogied his head, then set him back in the chair and gave him the rest of her sandwich. "Eat this." She turned to Loah. "He's an amoeba, but he's right about one thing." She pulled a breath and slowly let it out. "I finally did it. I'm running away."

"You mean..." Loah took a step back. "From home?"

"Where else do you run away from?"

Zeke tried to stand up, but Ellis flattened her hand on his head and pushed him back down. He howled.

"I hate you, Squirrel Smith!"

"Shut up!" Ellis snapped. She blushed, freckles drowning in a sea of red.

Squirrel?

"Ignore him," Ellis told Loah again. "He makes a doorknob look smart."

"A birdbrain and a squirrel brain! And you're both possum butts!"

Zeke jumped up, knocking over the chair. He was trying to act tough, but his hair had lost its spike and his ears were pink as seashells. He was just a boy trying his best not to cry. He swung back up into the maple tree and huddled in the crook of a branch.

Loah turned to Ellis. Who looked at Zeke, then the house, then her feet, where her big toe wiggled. At last, reluctantly, she turned her dark eyes to Loah.

"Squirrel's my real name," she said.

CHAPTER EIGHTEEN

They sat side by side on the next-to-bottom (not rotten) back step. When Ellis bent her head, her hair fell forward clumpily, and Loah could see it needed a shampoo.

"Squirrel Smith, that's me." She fingered the hem of her faded denim jacket, and Loah saw that it was embroidered with a garden of flowers. "When my mother was having me, she looked out the parlor window and saw a squirrel burying a nut. It looked so serious and determined, she said, but soon as its work was done, it started playing, climbing to the top of the shed and leaping through the air." Ellis let her finger rest on a yellow flower shaped like a heart. "My mother thought to herself, the squirrel knows how to work in the earth like a human, but it wants to soar through the air like a bird, too. Right then she decided my name." Ellis shook her head. "I was really small when I was born. PopPop—my grandfather— he added the Little part, and it stuck."

Little Squirrel. L.S. *Ellis.*

"Soon as I'm legal," Ellis went on, "I'm changing it. Maybe to Samantha or Melissa or even Ellis. I didn't decide yet. But no way I'm going through life named after an animal."

"But . . . you're not really. You're named after . . . after an idea. The idea of an animal."

Every flower stitched on Ellis's jacket was different. Some had rounded leaves. Others were pointy or feathery. Some had big show-off blooms, and others were shy, closed-up buds. Whoever had embroidered them knew a lot about flowers.

A robin began to sing. Robins are mostly known for being signs of spring, but they have one of the most beautiful songs of all backyard birds. The notes string together like bright beads on a silky cord. Close your eyes to listen, and you might find yourself wishing you were a robin so you could sing back.

"My mother named me for an animal, too," Loah said.

"I never heard of an animal called loah."

"It's a bird. But it's at risk of being extinct. It's on the International Union for Conservation of Nature's Red List. You can look it up on their website."

"You mean if we had internet I could."

"Oh."

"Your mother named you for something extinct?"

"She hopes not. That's why she's still in the Arctic. She's on a one-woman expedition to find the loah bird and protect it."

Ellis mulled this over. "The loah must be really special."

"Mama thinks all birds are."

"My mother loves birds, too. The kind that live here, I mean. She's never been to the Arctic, that's for sure."

The robin sang one last note, and the yard grew quiet.

"Your mother must be a very strong person," Ellis said then. "Strong and brave."

"She is." Loah felt a surge of pride. "She really is. She never gives up. If anyone can find and save the loah bird, it's her. Only . . . I miss her. It's been sixty-seven days now, and I still don't know when she'll be home."

"Our mother's brave, too," Zeke called down from his perch in the tree. "She can't help what happened to her."

"What?" Loah looked at Ellis. "What happened?"

"Your house is so big." Ellis jumped off the step. She craned her neck, pointing. "Nobody would even notice if I stayed here awhile. I could sleep in that tower. At night I'd sneak down to your room so we could have a sleepover. In the morning I'd sneak back up."

"It's a turret," said Loah, glancing up nervously. Its witch-hat roof gleamed dully in the sun. "And I couldn't let you stay there. It's . . ." She bit her tongue to keep from saying *haunted*. "Unstable."

"It looks haunted," said Zeke. "I bet there's skeleton bones up there."

"There must be lots of other places in your house to hide," said Ellis, ignoring him.

This was why she'd come. Why she'd worn her jacket and why her backpack bulged as if it held everything she owned. Ellis had run away, hoping Loah would help her.

"I'll tell PopPop," said Zeke. "He'll turn you inside out."

"If you rat on me, I'll kill you so dead you . . ." Ellis faltered. "So dead." Her head dipped. So did Loah's heart.

"Ellis." Loah stood up. "Is your mother all right?"

Ellis moved away to sit on Loah's swing. Curling her thin fingers around the ropes, she pushed off with one foot. Pumped.

"Last fall, Mama and PopPop were in the barn trying to move a piece of equipment. It was an old piece of junk he should've got rid of long ago, except PopPop never gets rid of anything. We live in a scrap yard." She kicked her legs out, swinging higher. "The piece of junk fell and crushed her leg and damaged her nerves, and they never got all the way better. It's hard for her to walk. Mostly she uses a wheelchair."

"Oh no! Ellis!"

"The medical bills wiped us out, and she can't help with the goats and garden like she used to. So the rest of us have more chores than ever, but there's no keeping up. And PopPop? I think he blames himself for the accident. You know about black holes?" She swung even higher, feet punching the air. "How they suck in anything that comes near and destroy it?"

Loah didn't see how the story could get worse, but then it did.

"I try to help. I do my chores and I study and I keep Mama's bird feeders full and...But sometimes I get so sick of it, I can't stop myself saying mean things. Really mean things."

"She does!" Zeke jumped down from the tree. "She's mean as a snake!"

"Then PopPop hollers, and Mama tells him, *Hush—Little Squirrel doesn't mean it,* and that makes me feel guilty so I say, *Yes I do!*" Ellis stopped pumping, and the swing began to slow. "Then this crybaby here starts blubbering, and Bully howls, and I really am sorry, but it's not like being sorry helps anything. So see? It's better for everybody if I just run away."

Zeke grabbed one of the swing's ropes, yanking it crooked. Ellis jumped off and caught him in a headlock.

"You gotta come home." He flailed his fists. "You gotta, Squirrel!"

"Shut up," said Ellis, her voice suddenly weary. She set her brother on the swing, then squeezed in beside him. He quieted, just the way Aquaman had in the meadow. She rested her chin on top of his head, murmuring something Loah couldn't hear.

A strong big sister with her arm around a sad little brother—they reminded Loah of something. What was it? A movie or a book or . . . No. It was Theo and Miss Rinker, abandoned by their mother on the orphanage steps.

"The day I met you, I was running away. I meant to go someplace really far, where they'd never find me." Ellis looked at Loah over the top of her brother's head. Her eyes were black seeds. "But then . . . there you were, at the bottom of the driveway. And something about you . . ." Her dark eyes flicked away. "It sounds weird but . . ."

"What? Tell me."

"You were like some sign that life wasn't all bad. That the world had good things in it, too. Happy things and funny things and interesting things and things I didn't even know anything about yet. It was like you showed up to remind me. And then . . ." She shook her head. "You came back! Just like I hoped you would. Nobody ever comes back to our house, not if they can help it. But you did. So I thought . . . maybe . . ."

When Ellis looked at Loah now, her eyes had begun to shine with that gleaming expectancy, the hope that Loah was who Ellis thought she was.

Loah didn't know what to say. So often in life she didn't know what to say, or was afraid that what she wanted to say was not what others wanted to hear, so that it had become much easier and safer to say nothing. Yet now when she said nothing, the light in Ellis's eyes dimmed. That spark faded away, as if she was realizing that

Loah was just any old person, not someone with a hidden patch of gold.

Loah couldn't stand to have Ellis look at her that way.

"Ellis, guess what? It's the same for me. You showed up now just when I was feeling . . . I'm here all alone and I don't know what to do! Theo's having heart surgery. Right now." Before Loah could stop herself, she added, "He could die."

"Die?" Zeke sat up straight. Ellis jumped off the swing.

"Loah," she said, "what are you talking about?"

Where to begin? Loah told them how the Rinkers had taken care of her for as long as she could remember, how she still slept with the baby blanket Miss Rinker once wrapped her in, how Theo had made that wooden swing, how he'd taught her to skip, though she wasn't good at it, how he'd knocked over a display of bargain beach balls and they'd discovered his heart was leaky, how Miss Rinker refused to let her come to the hospital—

"Stop. Stop right there." Ellis held up her hand. Her scowl was fierce. Great-horned-owl-defending-its-owlets fierce. "What do you mean, she wouldn't let you come?"

"She said I'd be in the way." Loah swallowed. "She said I'd be one more thing to worry about."

"You? How could *you* ever be in the way? You're helpful, thoughtful, and very smart." Ellis's scowl grew so ferocious, even Zeke looked scared. "I can't believe she left you here all alone. That's cruel and hard-hearted."

"She doesn't mean to be cruel. It's just how she is."

"What does your mother say?"

"She doesn't know about any of it."

"This is messed up. This is not how families work. When

Mama had her accident we all went and waited together, even Zeke." Ellis pulled her brother off the swing. "We'll go with you. Get your bike."

"But . . . What? You mean to the hospital? It's so far."

"We'll go with you," Ellis repeated, hoisting her backpack.

"But Miss Rinker—"

"That stinker is wrong. You can't listen to her. You need to be there."

"Only dead fish go with the stream!" Zeke pumped his fist.

Cheer cheer cheer! A cardinal's song broke the silence. A jay landed at Loah's feet and twisted its head indignantly.

Go, it screeched. *What are you waiting for?*

In the kitchen, she took her helmet and backpack off the hooks. The CREW poncho hung there, too, and she slipped it over her head. At the last second, she opened the broom closet and found the other ponchos Miss Rinker had bought at Bargain Blaster. Grabbing two, she ran back outside.

"Here." She shook the yellow plastic squares, which unfolded in all their blinding glory. "They'll make you visible to passing cars."

Ellis looked dubious, but Zeke was delighted.

"Hit it, Crew!" He pulled on the poncho and grabbed his bike.

Moments later they were on the road, single file—first Ellis, then Zeke, and then, pedaling with all her might, desperately trying to keep her crew in sight, Loah.

CHAPTER NINETEEN

Much as they might want to, and wish to, and dream of it, girls cannot fly. Girls are not birds. Their bones aren't hollow and they don't have wings. Even girls far more adventurous than Loah (that would be most girls) are forced to obey the law of gravity.

So Loah's bike probably didn't lift off the ground, though they got to the hospital so fast, she'd have sworn it did.

The hospital was on the opposite side of town. Not to mention atop a hill. By the time they arrived and got off their bikes, she walked on legs of rubber. Her throat was so parched she could hardly speak.

"Have a drink." Zeke pulled Loah's THANKS FOR BEING YOU water bottle out of his backpack.

She took a long swallow, and he grabbed it back. Ellis was headed for the doors.

"You better not come in," said Loah. "Miss Rinker is going to be furious enough that I disobeyed her."

"Rinker stinker blinker finker." Zeke flapped his yellow plastic wings. The poncho came almost to his feet. "Throw her in the clinker."

"Are you sure you'll be okay?" asked Ellis.

Loah pulled her phone from her snowy owl backpack. "What's your number? I'll call you when I know how he is."

"We don't have a phone."

Loah had never met anyone who didn't have a phone.

"If you want," she said, "you can go back to my house. I'll meet you there."

"No," said Zeke. "She's gotta come home now."

"Never mind about us," said Ellis. "You need to go in."

"Thank you for getting me here," Loah said.

The hospital doors slid apart automatically. The air-conditioning was set on Arctic. Loah immediately began to shiver. A woman with a face round and rosy as a baby doll's sat at the information desk. Her eyes widened as Loah staggered toward the desk in her poncho.

Only days ago, Loah would have hated asking for help. Actually, she still hated it, but she was getting better at doing things she was no good at (if that makes sense). When she asked where the surgery waiting room was, the rosy-faced woman replied with complicated directions.

"Thank you," Loah said, and blundered off on her rubber legs.

She had expected the hospital to be even worse than school—a necessary but highly unpleasant place. To her surprise it was bright and orderly, with paintings on the walls and pots of silk flowers at every turn. But she'd been too nervous to pay close attention to the directions and quickly got lost. She passed other visitors, carrying balloons and bouquets. A couple with red-rimmed eyes shuffled by. The man clutched a large white handkerchief, and Loah tried not to think how a white flag was the sign of surrender. She turned down another hallway, by now hopelessly confused.

"You all right, dumpling?"

A woman in a smock printed with kittens and puppies stood before her. Her face was so kind, Loah was in sudden danger of weeping. Why should kindness make her go to pieces? She reached up and pulled on her earlobes, a trick that sometimes kept her from crying.

"I'm looking . . . looking for the surgery waiting room."

"This way."

In no time at all, they came to a large room with row upon row of chairs, all occupied by people with drawn, anxious faces. The carpeting was well worn, as if many feet had paced back and forth here.

"You see your family?" the kindly woman asked.

Miss Rinker sat on the other side of the room. Had she shrunk even more? Her feet barely touched the carpet. She looked like a pile of sticks buttoned into a sweater.

"Yes," said Loah.

"Good luck, dumpling." The woman squeezed her hand and bustled away.

Miss Rinker's neck was bent. Her hat was in her lap. She might have been asleep, except she was stroking her hat's snow goose feather over and over, the way Loah stroked the silky edge of her baby blanket. Poor Miss Rinker! There was no keeping busy here. If any place in the world could make a person feel helpless, here it was.

Loah started across the room just as the door to the area where medical things happened opened. A tall doctor in blue scrubs, with puffy blue covers on his shoes, strode in. When he pulled his mask down, he was as dazzlingly handsome as if he'd stepped out of a TV hospital show.

"Rinker," he called, looking around the room. "Rinker?"

Miss Rinker stiffened as if electrocuted. She raised her hand and tried to stand, but her knees locked and she tottered. Loah was just in time to catch her.

CHAPTER TWENTY

$\int$he'll be fine, don't worry." A nurse with silver earrings shaped like hands was leading Loah down yet another endless hallway. "Poor thing's dehydrated and exhausted, is all." They were in another part of the hospital, which was like a clown car, stuffed with more corridors and rooms than seemed possible. "By the way, who's here with you?"

"Theo and Miss Rinker. He had a leaky heart and they were very worried, more worried than anyone even told me, but he survived the surgery." Loah was so relieved, she said it again. "He survived."

"Right." The nurse nodded and her hand earrings merrily waved. "Someone who's not a patient, is what I mean."

Loah never lied unless necessary. For example, if things were so complicated that a stranger—even a nice stranger—could never understand. Even then, she tried not to lie.

"My mother, Dr. Anastasia Londonderry, is an ornithologist specializing in birds of the Arctic tundra, where rising temperatures are radically changing the landscape and making life difficult for many species. Plus, the thawing permafrost is a source of green-house gas emissions, so it's a vicious circle."

"For goodness' sake," said the nurse.

"My mother's not a patient."

"I should hope not. That sounds like very important work."

"It is."

"Here we are."

Long rows of beds were separated by what looked like shower curtains. The nurse pushed one back to reveal Miss Rinker. Who barely made a bump beneath the covers, but looked much better than when she'd collapsed in Loah's arms. Her cheeks had color and her eyes were open.

"You *are* here," she said. "I was afraid I'd suffered a hallucination."

"Miss Rinker, how do you feel?" Loah asked. "Are you better?"

"I *knew* I didn't hallucinate. My brain is a steel trap."

A tube ran from a plastic bag hung on a pole to a needle taped to the crook of her arm. Something that resembled a stapler clamped her finger. Do not go woozy, do not go woozy, Loah begged herself. Miss Rinker narrowed her eyes, but before she could say anything more, the curtain swept back again to reveal the made-for-TV doctor. He was smiling, which made him even handsomer.

"You're looking much better!" he told Miss Rinker. "Your granddaughter made a great catch. Probably saved you from a concussion." He high-fived Loah, then folded his arms across his brawny chest. "More good news—we're pleased with how Mr. Rinker is doing. His vitals are fine, and he tolerated anesthesia well. We need to go one day at a time, but for now, there's cause to celebrate."

The doctor smiled again, radiating handsomeness.

"We medical people hate to admit it, but there's a limit to what we can do. The rest is up to the patient." He patted Loah's shoulder. "People say, I'm dying to do this or I'm dying to do that. But the real trick is to *live* for something! From the looks of things, Mr. Rinker has two excellent reasons to live. Good work, ladies." He patted Loah's shoulder again. "Nice poncho." With a jaunty thumbs-up, he went back out, pulling the curtain shut behind him.

Miss Rinker and Loah looked at each other. From beyond the curtain came voices, footsteps, the rattle of carts, but inside was like a cocoon.

It was one of those moments when anything you say will be clumsy and awkward and not what you meant at all. One of those moments when words become useless things. Even Miss Rinker, never at a loss for words, felt this, Loah could tell. She reached for the bony white hand. Miss Rinker curled her icy fingers around Loah's.

Then snatched them back.

"I told you not to come. I wish you hadn't."

Maybe this was the truth, but it was undeniably cruel, even for Miss Rinker.

She's wrong, Ellis said. *This is messed up. This is not how families work.*

"Miss Rinker—"

"You disobeyed me and now look. Just look."

"Miss Rinker, you're in bed!"

"Don't tell me where I am!"

"You were so dehydrated and exhausted you collapsed. It's a good thing I was there."

Loah had never spoken to Miss Rinker this way and could

hardly believe she was doing it now. But Ellis's voice was whispering that she was helpful and thoughtful. Telling her that families stuck together, no matter what. And though Loah had never before used that word for Miss Rinker and Theo, she understood now that they *were* her family, not in the same way Mama was, but still. If anything happened to either of them, she didn't know what she'd do. Though she didn't know how to put into words this thought, a thought that was startling but also somehow wasn't, as if it were a vast continent or a glittering galaxy that had been there all along, just waiting to be found—though she didn't know how to tell Miss Rinker any of this, especially since Miss Rinker was staring at her as if she'd sprouted a second head, one with horns, Loah tried.

"Miss Rinker, this has all been too hard. You tried to do too much, and you tried to do it all alone. You needed help." She swallowed. "In fact, you needed me."

Miss Rinker bared her dentures. She rapped her bed table so hard, everything on it jumped in alarm.

"You are a child!"

"I know. I needed you, too."

Slowly, like a chunk of ice in the sun, Miss Rinker melted back against her pillow. Her cheeks sagged and she fumbled for the tissue box.

"That is exactly the point," Miss Rinker said.

Loah handed her the box, and she pulled out a tissue.

"You're not supposed to see me like this. It's my job to be strong and take care of you. Not the other way around." She plucked tissue after tissue until she had an enormous wad, which she pressed to her nose and blew with an earsplitting honk.

Loah could have said she was sorry, but remember how she felt about lying? Instead she said, "Not so hard." Which was what Miss Rinker always told her.

"Oh for heaven's sake." Miss Rinker sniffled. "First you disobey me, then you cruelly point out that I'm flat on my back, then you instruct me on how to blow my own nose." She blew it again, more gently. "I hardly know who you are. I have lost my bearings."

Ferdinand Magellan, thought Loah. Women in space. Explorers of unknown territory.

Miss Rinker balled the tissue in her fist. She sank deeper into her pillow.

"That cocky young doctor thinks you're my granddaughter," she said with a sigh.

"I don't mind," Loah said.

Miss Rinker grabbed another tissue.

A bird knows what it needs. Food, shelter, companions. A sturdy nest, a partner in song.

But a human can be slow to discover what her heart wants. Sometimes she doesn't know till the moment it appears before her.

The next doctor who examined Miss Rinker decided to keep her for forty-eight hours to make sure she got sufficient fluids and rest. Once she was unhappily settled in her room, and had repeated her voluminous directions for staying alone, and had ordered Loah to be very careful on her bike and to call the moment she was safely home, they at last said goodbye. When Loah went to the nurses' station and asked to see Theo, the nurse told her he was in recovery, no children allowed. She promised Loah that both Rinkers were in good hands, and then, after that, there was nothing more for Loah to do. After getting lost several more times, she found her way to the lobby and stumbled out the automatic front doors.

By now it was late afternoon, and the sun sent long shadows slanting across the ground. Near the door, surrounded by a flower bed, stood a stone angel. Her wings were spread, as if she'd just landed, and her arms were outstretched as if to protect the two people slumped together on the bench before her.

Two people wearing radioactive-yellow plastic, their heads together and eyes closed.

A rumple of friends.

"You're still here!"

Ellis lurched upright. "What happened? How is he?"

"They think he'll be all right. Miss Rinker, too."

As Loah explained, a pigeon flew down to perch on the angel's wing. Cooing, it preened in the afternoon sun, showing off its iridescent feathers, so superior to the dull stone.

"I can't believe you stayed," Loah said.

"We didn't want you to be alone in case . . . you know," Ellis said.

Loah snuggled between them. Zeke, still half asleep, let his head fall against her arm. Drool glued his poncho to his little-boy cheek. Above them the angel spread her wings and the pigeon softly cooed. The three of them filled the bench just right, like passengers in a boat or eggs in a nest, and they sat there till the gathering shadows told them it was time to leave.

This time they rode slowly, Zeke in front, Ellis and Loah side by side. Ellis hadn't told Loah whether she'd changed her mind about running away, but Zeke acted as if his sister was coming home with him. Loah rode along, not ready to say goodbye. At the fork in the road, they all went left, and when at last they came to the meadow and the dusty driveway, they all stood on their pedals and rode to the crest of the hill, where one final sign declared in foot-high letters: THIS CONSTITUTES YOUR FINAL WARNING.

Loah gazed down into a green hollow. She saw:

Dozens of goats in a big, fenced-in pen. (Was that Aquaman, butting his stubborn little head against the chicken wire?) A faded red barn. A washing machine with a chicken sitting on top. A target bristling with arrows. A trampoline. Piles of wood, piles of tires, piles of metal scrap. Piles of piles. Tarps covering unidentifiable mounds. Sheds—many sheds. What might be beehives. A pickup truck so rusty it seemed to be made of brown lace. Everywhere— wooden birdhouses of every size.

And a humans' house. Narrow and low, like a submarine sinking beneath the waves. A tattered banner hanging from a pole said ONLY DEAD FISH GO WITH THE STREAM. Flowers of every color, yellow and purple and white and red, bloomed around the house, and pink roses clambered up one side. A ramp, the kind made for wheelchairs, zigzagged to the front porch where Bully lay chomping what looked like a stegosaurus bone.

A marmalade-colored cat stepped daintily out of the grass and flopped over at Loah's feet. When she petted it, the cat slitted its eyes and purred as if no one in the whole history of the world had ever petted it so well.

"Hope the stinkers are okay, birdbrain! See you later!"

Poncho flapping, Zeke flew no-handed down the driveway. Bully dropped his bone. He scrambled to his feet, jaws sagging and eyes bugging. What was this weird, toxic-yellow cloud hurtling toward the house? An enemy! An enemy for sure. Bully commenced doing what he did best: barking his giant head off. Zeke dropped his bike, waved back at Loah and Ellis, then ran inside.

Loah braced for goodbye. She was already imagining another night alone in the empty—the very empty—house when Ellis rolled her bike backward, out of the sight of the house.

"PopPop's going to be so mad. At both of us, but especially me. We didn't do our chores, we took off without telling him...He'll say it's all my fault. I'm going to be..."

Her voice was like something dropping down a well. When Loah looked back, she saw Zeke stick his head out the front door, wave his arm frantically, and duck back inside.

The chicken flew down from the washing machine. More like tumbled—chickens were not good at flying. A chicken spent its life pecking in the dirt. It let humans steal its eggs, no problem. Still it was a bird, the same as a goshawk or an emu was. How could that be? What was the thing that made them all birds?

And why was Loah wondering that now?

Once before, she'd had the chance to help Ellis. Only she hadn't been ready, not then.

Now she couldn't be sure if it was Ellis she was helping—or herself.

"You can come to my house if you want," she said.

"What?" Ellis's eyes lit up like a hundred candles. Like a sky full of stars. "Are you sure? Because if Zeke tells PopPop I ran away—"

"If he comes, we'll hide."

Down in the hollow, Zeke ran out onto the porch, poncho flapping. He peered up at Loah, who shook her head and put a finger to her lips.

"Do you think we really could?" Ellis said. "Up in the tur-ret. No, not there, right? But somewhere. Are you sure it's okay?" She was already climbing on her bike. "Loah! Come on, we better hurry!"

She was helping someone run away from home. If you think Loah had ever, in her entire eleven and one half years of life, expected to do that, you just have not been paying attention.

CHAPTER TWENTY-ONE

One of Dr. Londonderry's bedtime stories was about two birds you'd never expect to be teammates.

"Peregrine falcons and red-breasted geese nest on the ground, the way most tundra birds do," she'd begin. "The falcon makes its nest and the geese build theirs all around it, like a village around a castle. When the falcon goes off hunting, the geese guard the eggs. If they spy a predator, they set up an enormous racket."

Here Loah's mother would do a deafening imitation of the red-breasted goose, complete with honking, hissing, and fiercely flapping wings. Loah would laugh, but her heart would quake, thinking of the eggs.

"The falcon hears the alarm and rushes back. Falcons can reach speeds of up to two hundred miles per hour, so it doesn't take long. She swoops down, vicious beak and talons at the ready, and attacks the predator. It flees for its life, and the eggs of all the birds are saved!"

Loah would hug her pillow in relief.

"People think nature's all about competition and survival of the fittest. But it's just as much about cooperation. The falcon and the goose are only one wonderful example." Mama would lean back with a radiant smile. "The real 'world wide web' is how interdependent we all are, right down to the microorganisms in the soil and the bacteria in our guts. We humans could learn everything we need to know from the natural world, if we'd only pay attention."

Riding home with Ellis now, Loah had time to contemplate what she'd gotten herself into. If Zeke snitched...(And of course he would.) If PopPop came looking for Ellis...(And he would, wouldn't he?) She remembered Zeke asking, *Do you know what buckshot is?* Loah tried to formulate a plan, but it had been a long, hard day, and her brain was unused to planning anything beyond which knitting project to do next.

Home—there it was at last! Its heavy, mud-brown stone, its three chimneys, its crooked turret hanging on for dear life. Its noble trees and long gravel driveway...where Inspector Wayne J. Kipper stood with his neck craned so far back his cap had fallen off.

Following the inspector's gaze, Loah saw that the vulture had returned. It shifted from foot to foot, like a gravedigger impatient for the hearse to deliver the corpse. (Which, thank goodness, she'd only seen in movies, not real life.)

"Stay back! You got a bird of prey on your roof!" Inspector Kipper waved his arms as they got off their bikes. Did he mean to protect them, or for them to protect him?

A scraping sound on the roof made the vulture dance sideways, then spread its wings and take off. In what was a perfect example of bad timing, another slate came loose from the roof. It shot off the edge, hung in the air, then knifed down, slicing the branch of a tender young sapling clean off.

"Guillotine," said the inspector.

He picked up his cap and fanned his face. His bald spot shone. His so-called beard looked more pathetic than ever. Also, two buttons on his shirt were undone, revealing a Superman T-shirt underneath. There is something sad about grown-ups wearing superhero stuff.

With Ellis by her side, Loah almost felt sorry for him.

"Let me guess," he said. "Dr. Londonberry isn't home. What's the excuse this time?"

So much for feeling sorry for him.

"Exactly who wants to know?" Ellis stepped forward.

The inspector widened his eyes. "And who might you be, young lady?"

"I asked you first." Ellis scowled the way she had when she heard Miss Rinker had left Loah home alone. It was a scowl of outrage and defiance, the scowl of someone who knows the rest of the world is wrong and she's right and she'll happily bite your head off to settle things once and for all. In other words, a completely un-Ellis look. Where had she learned to make a face like that?

"I'm Wayne J. Kipper, here in my official capacity as senior housing inspector for this city." He hooked a thumb into his utility belt, where, Loah saw, he had a new can of The Terminator. Turning to her, he said, "In point of fact, I made a personal sacrifice to come here after normal working hours. I was hoping to finally catch your mother. But I see you've been left alone again."

"Excuse me?" said Ellis. "Alone? What does that make me?"

"In point of fact," the inspector repeated, ignoring her, "I've never once seen a single adult on these premises."

He frowned at Loah. She couldn't tell if it was a frown of anger or concern, not that it made any difference. A frowning inspector was not a good thing.

"I'm beginning to think," he said, "that you are an unsupervised minor."

The vulture, its wings a flattened V, circled the roof several times before it landed in the precise spot where it had been. It grunted as if surprised they were still there.

"I'm fine," Loah said. "I've got Ellis, as you can see. And I've got the Rinkers. They live here and take excellent care of me."

"May I speak to them?"

"They're not home. At the moment."

This was not going well. Loah's weak eye tugged toward the roof, where the vulture hunched its shoulders and paced back and forth, issuing more repulsive grunts. The inspector was still studying Loah. He bit his lower lip. Did *he* actually look a little sorry for *her*?

"What's up with those ponchos?" he asked, and when she didn't answer, his frown deepened. "Since my last inspection, things have further deteriorated. A significant chunk of masonry is missing from that tower."

"Turret," said Ellis. "It's a turret. You'd think an official housing inspector would know the difference. Not to mention, it's *derry* not *berry*." By now her scowl was man-eating. Loah knew Ellis meant well, but it was possible she wasn't helping.

"I know my house needs work," Loah said. "My mother will fix things as soon as she can."

"My office has sent numerous notices over the past six months. She's never answered a single one."

Loah suddenly remembered that official-looking envelope she'd laid on top of all the others on her mother's desk.

"Loah's mother is very busy doing things that really matter," said Ellis. "Not like some other people."

The inspector, continuing to ignore her, produced a folder.

"The city gives people ample opportunity to comply. But there comes a time when time runs out." He shuffled through the papers in the folder, pulled one out, and began to read.

"'All dwelling structures and all parts thereof, both exterior and interior, shall be maintained in good repair and safe order, and shall be capable of performing the function for which such structure or part of any feature thereof was designed or intended to be used. One that is so damaged, decayed, dilapidated, unsanitary, unsafe or vermin-infested that it creates a hazard to the health, welfare, or safety of the occupants or of the public shall be deemed uninhabitable.'" He looked up. "In point of fact, that is our official city housing code."

"But—my house isn't uninhabitable. I inhabit it."

"I'm here off the clock to try to personally ensure the property owner receives her final notice."

Final? That had a highly unpleasant sound. When the inspector held out an envelope, Loah didn't take it. Instead, Ellis did.

And ripped it in half.

"Destroying official documents is punishable by fine!"

"You think you can scare me?" Ellis dropped the pieces on the ground. "Ha!"

A downy woodpecker landed on the trunk of a nearby sycamore

tree. It began to drum, *rat a tat tat*. Downy woodpeckers are specially adapted to repeatedly smacking their beaks against hard surfaces. Their skulls contain next to no fluid, so their brains don't slosh around, and they can drill into trees with a force a thousand times the force of gravity. (Also, they have barbed and sticky tongues, but that's another matter.)

Inspector Kipper eyed the bird yet stood his ground. Turning his back on Ellis, he addressed Loah.

"You seem like a nice, well-behaved child. Why are you hanging around with a troublemaker like her?"

"Please don't insult my friend."

"I'm trying to help you. Considering your mother doesn't seem big in the mothering department."

"And definitely don't insult my mother!"

Inspector Kipper picked up the torn envelope and handed the pieces to Loah. Fed up was how he looked. He had *had* it.

"I don't know where the heck Dr. Londonberry-derry is, or if she even exists, to tell you the truth. What I do know is she's got five working days to reply to this notice or suffer the consequences." He puffed his chest, straining the buttons on his shirt so the sorry Superman symbol peeked out. "You shouldn't be in the middle of this. It's your mother's responsibility, not yours. She has neglected her duties as a homeowner. Unfortunately, it looks like she neglects her duties as a parent as well."

"I said, do not insult my mother!" Loah cried.

Rat a tat, went the bird-jackhammer. *Screech!* A pair of jays did a synchronized swoop. The inspector fingered his can of The Terminator, but when Loah cried, "Don't you dare!" he instead shielded his head with his clipboard and stalked to his car.

"The law is the law," he called over his shoulder. "Anyone who thinks they're above it is in for a big surprise." He jumped into his car and reversed out the drive.

When Loah turned around, the vulture was gone. She hadn't heard it flap its wings or felt its shadow pass overhead. It had just vanished, like a ghost.

CHAPTER TWENTY-TWO

Every nestling loves its nest, whether it's tidy or slapdash, perched on the edge of a perilous cliff or tucked in a potted plant on a backyard deck. Some hatch in nests stolen from other birds, yet what do they care? Every baby bird loves the place its mother lays it.

But then, it doesn't know any better, does it?

Loah, it hardly bears repeating, loved her home. Up till now, though, she'd rarely shared it with anyone except her mother and the Rinkers. As she led Ellis inside, she suddenly felt shy. What if Ellis thought it was spooky? What if it gave her goose bumps?

She didn't need to worry. Ellis loved the house. She loved the stag-head chandelier. She loved the faded carpet with the roses like chubby pink faces. She loved the kitchen with its black-and-white-checkered floor tiles and big, comfy E-Z Boys. She opened and closed the doors of all the dusty, unused rooms, whistling under her breath. In the library, she gaped at all the books and admired the ones Mama had written. She stood Loah's school photos, which Loah had laid facedown, upright on the desk and examined them like artifacts from another civilization. She saved her highest compliments for Loah's fish. Of all the animals the

Smiths owned, they had no fish. She couldn't believe Loah hadn't named it yet.

I agree! The fish did a quick lap around its bowl.

Loah was about to call Miss Rinker and say she'd made it home when she noticed that the phone's message light was blinking. She pressed the button.

"Sweetie? Are you there?" Her mother's voice always squeaked when she was excited, but Loah had never heard it pitch so high and breathless as now. "I want to—" *Click.*

"Was that her?" Ellis asked. "Was that your mom? Why'd she hang up?"

"She got cut off. That happens a lot. She'll call back when she can."

Loah should have been happy. She was happy, wasn't she? Her mother hadn't fallen down a crevasse, been mauled by a polar bear, or gotten deathly sick from drinking bad water! All this time, as Loah had wondered and worried about her, Mama had been just fine. She'd been better than fine. Only one thing in this world, Loah knew, could make her mother sound as happy as she did.

The loah bird. Mama must have found it at last.

Loah the girl sank into Mama's chair.

Ellis chose a book and took it to the window seat. Loah called Miss Rinker to say she was home, that she'd heard from her mother, and that, yes, everything was fine. To Loah's relief, Miss Rinker sounded too tired to ask many questions.

After she hung up, Loah began to sift through the papers on the desk. Besides the envelope she'd set there, she found two other notices from the Department of Housing. The most recent one was, of course, unopened, but the other two had been taken from their envelopes, then stuffed back in. Mama had read them before her trip and ignored them.

Loah read the list of violations. It was long. *Long.* Some were serious—the turret, for example, and the roof, and the trees with dead limbs—but others not so much. Cracked windows, the rotten back step, chipped paint. It wouldn't have been too hard or expensive to fix them, if Dr. Londonderry had paid attention. If she'd taken more care. If she'd thought about the house as a place to live, instead of a place to fly away from.

Loah opened the envelope Ellis had torn in two. Fitting the pieces of the letter together, she tried to make sense of it. Though it contained numerous confusing words and phrases like "noncompliance" and "pursuant to Code 762, Section 17," she was able to zero in on one sentence, the one containing the words "will thereby be summoned to appear in municipal court."

There might also have been something about "failure to appear resulting in warrant for arrest." In fact, there definitely was. But there was only so much scary news her brain could process at one time.

The inspector was a horrible man. He didn't know a tower from a turret. He didn't like trees. Who didn't like trees? He'd terminate innocent creatures who got in his way, which was unforgivable. He had even insulted Ellis, when all she was doing was sticking up for Loah.

Sticking up for her, like family.

Unfortunately, it looks like she neglects her duties as a parent as well.

The final notice trembled in Loah's hands. Glancing at Ellis, who'd tossed the book aside and was gazing out the window, she walked over to the bookshelves and ran a finger down the spine of *The Egg: Nature's Greatest Feat of Engineering.* Once she'd asked Mama how a baby bird knew when it was time to hatch.

"Her baby tooth—her little egg tooth—touches the inside of her shell," Dr. Londonderry said. "Her instincts tell her she's outgrown it."

Hatching was strenuous work, she explained. The hatchling used her tooth to tap at the shell, again and again—pipping, this was called—till at last, after a long time, it made a tiny crack. This took so much energy and strength, afterward the poor chick collapsed from the effort. She had to rest and recuperate. Not for long, though. Soon enough, she was back on the job, chipping her way toward the light.

Loah spun away from the shelf. She told herself Mama didn't know how wrong things here had gone. How could she? Mama was too busy. Her work was too important. It was impossible to think of work more important than hers.

Loah told herself that Mama didn't know Theo had heart trouble—though why didn't she, considering how old and frail he was? Her mother didn't know about the housing department closing in—though why didn't she, since she'd ignored all the warnings they'd sent? She didn't know about the evil-omen vulture—though if she did, she'd sing its praises for sure.

Loah told herself all this.

She told herself that Mama didn't know how much she'd been alone, except for her faithful, nameless fish. Which, come to think of it, her mother also didn't know about.

Her mother didn't even know about Ellis. Didn't know that Loah had helped someone run away from home and was glad about it.

When you came down to it, her mother knew nothing about Loah's life right now.

Why didn't she?

Because.

Face the truth, Loah told herself. Even if it hurts. Especially if it hurts.

Mama loves the birds as much as she loves you.

Maybe... more.

It hurt. Loah felt cracks running through her every which way. Her world was breaking into pieces and could never be whole again. It hurt.

Ellis had her nose pressed to the window screen. Beyond her, out among the trees, dusk was sweeping all the shadows together. The birds were quiet, their evening songs sung. As if she felt Loah looking at her, Ellis turned her head.

"I'm really glad I'm here," she said softly. "But I'm worried about Zeke. I shouldn't have left him to face PopPop alone. And my mother... I know I said how upset she gets me, but it's not her fault she had that accident. She can't help it that she's not strong and happy, the way she used to be, before. It's not really her I'm angry at. It's..." She looked out the window. "It's all the stuff I can't change. The things I wish were different but can't be."

Sometimes, when you're hurt yourself, helping someone else is the only way to feel better. Sharing the hurt thins it out and takes away its power.

Loah sat next to Ellis on the window seat.

"I know," she whispered. "I know what you mean."

Outside, the spaces between the trees shrank till they disappeared in the velvety dark. Inside, Loah began to feel different. When she drew a breath, her lungs had more room for air. Her arms and legs felt looser and easier, as if her bones and muscles belonged to her in a new way. The world somehow had more space and light, even though by now it was full dark outside. Beside her, Ellis's stomach suddenly growled so ferociously they both jumped, then looked at each other and laughed.

"Do you like frozen pizza?" Loah asked.

Miss Rinker wouldn't mind her using the stove alone, she told herself, which probably wasn't true, but oh well. They ate the pizza while sitting on Loah's bed and watching *One and Only Family* on her laptop.

"This is so dumb," Ellis said, then immediately looked apologetic.

"That's okay," said Loah. "It *is* dumb."

"I think it's all right to like dumb things, even if you know they're dumb. PopPop likes country music, which is so corny and terrible, but some of the songs choke me up." Ellis shook her head. "Dumb," she said, smiling.

At Ellis's house they used a generator, and they ran out of hot water all the time. Here, the plumbing was unreliable, but tonight it decided to cooperate and let Ellis take a long shower. She came back to Loah's room trailing a cloud of flowery steam, her skin pink and her hair silky as ribbons. Her toes were wrinkled, and the big one wriggled happily. She pulled a clean, faded T-shirt from her backpack, which also contained a sack of cookies, dense with nuts and raisins, and a mason jar of homemade grape juice, which tasted nothing like the watery store stuff Miss Rinker favored.

By now they were pretty sure PopPop wasn't coming, though who knew why. Ellis said maybe he couldn't start the pickup, which happened all the time. Or maybe her mother was having one of her bad spells and needed him. Or maybe . . . She shook her head and grabbed the copy of *Women Spacefarers*, opening it to a photo of Valentina Vladimirovna Tereshkova, the first woman in space. Valentina had piercing brown eyes and a chest covered with medals. The book said that when she blasted off, she shouted, "Hey, sky, take off your hat! I'm coming!"

"So do you want to be an astronaut?" Ellis asked.

This was such a ridiculous question, Loah laugh-snorted, which made Ellis look confused, which made Loah realize, She actually, truly thinks I could blast off into the unknown.

"Miss Rinker says, 'What's so great about explorers? They only discover things that are already there.' But how are you supposed to discover something that isn't there? Besides, I didn't know you existed, but now that I know you do, well . . . I can't believe I didn't know all along."

At the bottom of Ellis's dark eyes, that spark kindled. It leaped across the space between them and kindled something in Loah, too. She could feel it flickering, shy at first, just a hint, just a glimmer, but then it caught and blazed, and warmth spread all through her. Ellis pushed her shiny, ribbony hair back from her face and smiled.

Loah smiled back. She held up the photo of the very first woman in space.

"Hey, sky, take off your hat! I'm coming!" they shouted together, and fell over laughing.

Sometime, deep in the night, Loah woke to hear the screech owl wailing like someone who'd died and come back to complain about it. Ellis wasn't in the bed. Loah pulled her scrap of baby blanket from under her pillow. Had Ellis changed her mind? Had she decided to go home?

"Did you hear that?"

Loah clicked on the bedside lamp and saw her, standing in the bedroom doorway.

"It's just an owl," Loah said in relief.

"Not that. Something else. I heard noises down the hall. Thumps." Ellis leaned out the door, listening. "I don't hear it now."

Climbing back into bed, Ellis noticed Loah's blanket. Loah felt her face go red with embarrassment. But Ellis reached down and pulled a knotty tangle of yarn from her backpack.

"My mother made it for me when I was born." She rolled her eyes, then set her blanket next to Loah's and smiled. "Hard to decide which looks worse."

"I think it's a tie."

Loah turned off the light and, holding their baby blankets, they snuggled back down and soon fell fast asleep.

A slumber of girls.

CHAPTER TWENTY-THREE

Loah's mother was home at last. She'd lost her keys (again) and was on the doorstep ringing the bell (which didn't work but somehow Loah heard). The entryway was heaped with piles of rubble and dead branches (how had they gotten inside?), which Loah had to scramble over. It took forever, and by the time she reached the door, it wasn't the front door at all but the door to the turret. She needed all her strength to open it and by the time she did, her mother's arms and head were covered in white feathers. In the middle of her face—a long black beak.

"Mama!" cried Loah as her mother beat her wings. "Wait!" Loah tried to catch her, but her mother lifted into the air. "Mama, no! You live here! Here!" Loah stretched her empty, so empty, arms toward the sky. "Come back!"

"Loah?" Ellis was shaking her shoulder. "Wake up. The phone's ringing."

Loah threw back the covers. She rushed along the corridor and down the stairs. She could hear the phone ringing but only faintly, like something about to give up and expire. She missed the last steps and tumbled onto her bum, but at last made it to the library, where she dived across her mother's desk and grabbed the phone.

"Hello?"

A passing breeze. A sigh. The beat of a single wing.

"Hello? Hello?"

Click.

Outside the birds were making a commotion, the way they did every morning, but today they were even more raucous than usual, as if they, too, were trying to wake her up to answer the phone. As she slowly climbed back upstairs, she felt her dream clinging to her like an ugly, sticky cobweb.

"Who was it?" Ellis was waiting at the top of the staircase.

"I was dreaming about my mother. A bad dream."

Ellis, face creased with sleep, waited patiently.

"And then she called. I could see it was her satellite phone number. But . . ."

At the end of the dim corridor, Loah could see the turret door, still shut tight.

"But?" prompted Ellis.

"She didn't say anything."

Loah shut her eyes. In her dream, she'd gotten to the front door—the turret door—too late. If only she'd opened it sooner, she could have kept her mother from becoming a small dot swallowed up by the vast sky. The dream was still so real her empty arms ached.

"Call her back," Ellis said.

"I'm only allowed to call in an emergency. It's a rule."

"Sometimes you need to break the rules."

They dressed, then carried the fishbowl down to the library, where Loah, for the first time in her life, dialed the programmed number. Ellis stood close, listening, too, as it rang and rang. Mama's message came on.

" 'Hope is the thing with feathers.' This is Dr. Anastasia Londonderry. I am literally and figuratively on top of the world!"

"Mama, it's me. Please call back."

As they sat waiting on the window seat, Loah told Ellis about her mother's other expeditions. The time she lost the tip of a finger to frostbite, the time her eyes swelled shut from the stings of vicious Arctic mosquitoes, the time she got hypothermia from falling into the sea.

"But she always survived," Loah said, trying to reassure them both. "She always came back okay."

The look on Ellis's face was anything but reassuring.

Call me, Loah thought. Call me call me call—

The phone rang again. Without looking Loah knew—knew with every bit of her capable of knowing anything—that it was Mama.

And it was.

"Mama!" This was suddenly the only word she knew. "Mama!"

"Oh, sweetie." A sighing sound, like a dying breeze. "I'm so glad to hear your voice."

Her mother's voice wasn't squeaky now. The opposite—it was muted and flattened in a way Loah didn't recognize.

"Mama? You sound funny."

Another sigh.

"Is it the loah?" she asked. "You found her, didn't you?"

When her mother didn't answer, she knew something was very wrong. Had a predator gotten the bird? Had her breeding ground

134

deteriorated too badly for her to nest? Sudden sadness clutched Loah's heart. If that small, plain bird with the tiny streak of gold—if she'd managed to survive in spite of everything, only to be lost . . . ? Lost forever? And if there'd been eggs? What would happen to them?

"Mama!" If she felt this sad, think what her mother was feeling! The loah was a ray of hope for all birds, for the Arctic, for the planet! Mama had risked so much to find it. Brave, hopeful Mama. The anger and hurt Loah had been feeling disappeared. "Mama, I'm so sorry. You did all you could."

"Oh, sweetie. I'll be all right. It's just . . . something's wrong with my primary covert."

The primary covert is part of a bird's wing. Loah must have heard wrong.

"You mean the loah bird's wing?"

"My poor arm. And my poor old Jeep."

"I don't understand. Could you explain? Mama?"

Ellis, freckles in a knot, stood close.

"I don't think I can fix it," Dr. Londonderry said.

Did she mean her Jeep? Her arm? Both? The blood beat up in Loah's ears.

"Mama, are you hurt?" When her mother didn't answer, she said, "Can you tell me where you are?"

"There's a ridge. A pond to the northeast, or no, maybe it's west . . ."

"Can't you tell? What does your GPS say?"

Her mother sighed.

Ellis put a hand on Loah's arm, which helped her keep her voice calm.

"Where's your personal locator beacon? Your PLB? You have it with you, don't you? Do you need to activate it?"

Crackle.

"Drat," muttered her mother, who never muttered. "This foolish phone..."

"You need to charge it."

"You're right. What if I got cut off from you again? I must charge it."

Click.

"Not now! Mama, don't hang up!"

But she was gone.

CHAPTER TWENTY-FOUR

Every year, the Arctic tern migrates from one polar region to the other, approximately twelve thousand miles each way. If Loah were a tern, she could have set her internal compass, spread her wings, and set off to find her mother.

But Loah, this Loah, was a girl.

"We need to get help," Ellis said, once Loah had explained. "We need to tell someone."

We. Such a small word. Such a big word.

"Miss Rinker and Theo are in the hospital," said Loah.

"I know. Who else is there?"

"Dr. Whitaker, but—"

"Who's he?"

Loah explained how he was her mother's boss at the university, how the two of them were forever arguing, how Dr. Whitaker said there was only enough time and money to rescue the most significant species, and how Dr. Londonderry believed every single species was significant.

"He'd say she was on a wild-goose chase. She isn't even supposed to be there." Loah pulled on her earlobes. She couldn't cry now. But she wanted to. She really wanted to. "When her team left she stayed on by herself. It's against all the rules. He'd be furious if he knew."

Something hit the upper windowpane with a soft thud. They ran to look. On the ground, a house sparrow lay perfectly still. Just a fledgling, its feathers still downy and gray.

"Don't be dead!" begged Loah. "Please, please don't be."

The bird didn't move.

"If only she'd come home!" she cried, knocking her fist on the window. "She should've come home!"

"Maybe," said Ellis. "Probably. But she didn't. She knew it was risky and still decided to stay. Loah, she really really, *really* wanted to find that bird."

Leaning her forehead against the window, Loah heard Mama whispering their favorite story.

You were due in two weeks . . . I was so sad and lonely. My heart was lost and I couldn't find it.

The little sparrow gave a shudder. Life flickered in its breast.

That unmistakable streak of gold, like a shining ray of hope. Like a promise that everything wasn't over, and the world was still a place brimming with surprise and wonder and beauty for the finding.

The sparrow twisted its head and opened its eyes. Up on its feet, it gave a hop. Another hop.

As soon as I saw you, I knew your name.

Cheep! Chirrup! A flap of fledgling wings, and the bird was in the air. If only she were a bird! If only she had instincts, instead of confused thoughts and feelings! Should Loah call Miss Rinker? But what could she do from the hospital? Dr. Whitaker was the one who'd know how to help, but Mama would hate for him to know, wouldn't she? Maybe she should wait for Mama to call again. Mama was always so strong—she always knew what needed to be done. Maybe Loah should keep trying to call her back? But Mama had sounded so weak, so confused, so not-Mama.

"Loah," said Ellis. Loah hadn't realized she was pacing in circles till Ellis suddenly blocked her path. "Your mother needs you."

Sometimes in life, not often but sometimes, a person says a thing that sets you vibrating, as if their words are the wind and you are a wind chime.

Mama needed her.

Trembling, Loah went to her mother's desk, found the number of the university office, drew a breath, and dialed.

"You have reached the Department of Mammalogy and Ornithology," said a recorded message. "Due to reduced summer hours, the office is closed. Please leave a message or try again later."

Now she remembered—Mama had said Dr. Whitaker was off on his own trek. She began pacing again, bumping into the little table with the bowl of sunflower seeds she'd set out back when she still believed Mama would be home soon. The seeds skittered under the furniture and down cracks in the floor.

"Later," she said. "What does that mean?"

Trying to think, trying to think. Mama hadn't called for three days—had she been hurt all that time? Alone and hurt? Loah couldn't stand to think of it, but she had to. Now that she'd decided to get help, she couldn't wait for later.

"I need to get to the university," she told Ellis. "Someone there will know how to get in touch with Dr. Whitaker. If only Miss

Rinker was here to take me! I don't think I can ride my bike that far. Maybe I could call a taxi? How much do you think that would cost? There's some money in the sugar—"

But Ellis was already out the door, calling over her shoulder, "Come on. I'll get us there."

CHAPTER TWENTY-FIVE

Along the straight main road, onto the crooked side road, left at the fork, and around the bend to the signs shouting KEEP OUT and TRESPASSERS WILL BE PROSECUTED OR WORSE, all the way to the crest of the dirt driveway. Below, all was still. The ONLY DEAD FISH GO WITH THE STREAM banner hung limp on its pole. An empty wheelchair stood on the porch, and a calico cat slept on a shed roof. The pickup was parked where it had been yesterday—where, from the looks of it, it had been parked for a century. Only one thing moved. Up on top of the old washing machine, Aquaman did a tap dance.

THIS CONSTITUTES YOUR FINAL WARNING

"Are you sure you want to do this?" Loah asked. "Aren't you going to get in a lot of trouble?"

"I already am." Ellis pushed off. As her bike bumped down the hill, she called back, "Stay there. I mean it. Don't come unless I give you a signal." At the house, she dropped her bike and disappeared inside.

It was so quiet. Too quiet. Like in a horror movie, just before the killer lunges out of the closet with his bloody knife or the brain-eating monster lurches over the hill.

Then.

Maybe the walls of the house didn't actually shake, but they should have. The front door blew open and Zeke bolted out. Incredibly, he was still wearing the poncho. Spying Loah on the crest of the hill, he raised his arms like a living emergency beacon.

"Sorry, birdbrain! I tried!"

Inside the house, the yelling got louder. And louder. Ellis's voice was mixed in there somewhere, like a flute in a hurricane. Something crashed to the floor, and there was a sudden silence. Somehow, this was louder than the yelling.

"Run for your life!" cried Zeke. As if to demonstrate, he tore across the yard and ducked behind the barn.

Usually, when something is so frightening a person's stomach churns and her knees go to jelly, she has to summon her courage.

More rarely, courage summons her.

Down the bumpy hill, bones rattling, brain capable of a single thought. *Help Ellis.*

Loah, you don't need to be told, was not athletic. She wasn't even very coordinated. So when her bike hit a pothole (where did that come from?) at the bottom of the drive, there was no way she could recover her balance. Worse. She was going so fast, her own momentum pitched her over the handlebars and hurled her face-first onto the ground. Where she lay, stunned and aching and afraid to move, as something began to nibble her T-shirt.

"Baa!" Aquaman nudged her with his heart-shaped nose. "Baa?"

The front door opened. Footsteps pounded the ramp. She kept her face down, hoping to become one with the ground, but all at once she felt herself lifted into the air. Like a feather, a dust mote, a thing that weighed nothing at all, she was lifted and set on her feet.

Mr. PopPop Smith was an enormous person. If Stonehenge were human—that kind of big. Loah was used to small, scraggly old people, not colossal ones with arm muscles the size of navel oranges. She tried to look past him, to see if Ellis was near, but he blocked the view. Trembling, Loah fixed her eyes on his sandaled feet, which had long, yellowish toenails. The talons of the turkey vulture flashed before her.

"PopPop!" Ellis was suddenly there, inserting herself between him and Loah. "Quit scaring her. I told you—she's my friend, and she's in trouble."

"I'll give you trouble!" he snarled. "Get your sorry self inside, Squirrel."

"If you'd just listened to me instead of breaking Mama's lamp—"

"That was an accident!"

"Loah needs help!"

"You made your brother lie! He told us you were with your cousins. There I was, trying to cut you some slack and let you have a little fun, only to find out you snuck off behind my back. You spent the night who knows where, with who knows who!"

"I didn't make Zeke lie, and if you'd just calm down, I could introduce Loah and you'd see she's—"

"I don't care if she's the Queen of England." He fixed Loah with a fierce scowl. "What kind of friend talks you into running away? No kind, that's what."

"It was *my* idea to go, PopPop. And my idea to come back. Her mother—"

"Get in the house and tell *your* mother you're sorry." Mr. Smith set his face inches from Loah's. "Off. My. Property. Now."

Somehow Ellis squeezed back between the two of them. Her face wore its man-eating scowl, and at last, to her astonishment, Loah realized where Ellis had learned it. Her face was a mirror of her grandfather's.

"You're always telling us the number one rule is think for ourselves—well, I am. I don't care how you punish me later, but you have to listen to me now." Ellis grabbed his big hand with both of hers. "Loah's mother is in serious trouble. We need to get to the university and find help."

"University?" He laughed. Not a nice laugh. "People with their fat heads up their fat butts. I needed help, last place I'd go was—"

"She's on an expedition to save an endangered bird." Loah found her voice at last. Aquaman was nibbling her shorts, and she rested a hand on his head to steady herself. "My mother is."

Mr. Smith continued to scowl, but it became a scowl of confusion. He was used to being in charge. He was like Miss Rinker, if Miss Rinker had biceps and talon toenails.

"Bird?" He shoved his hands in his pockets. "What kind of bird?"

"The loah bird."

"Never heard of it."

"She loves all kinds of birds." Loah pointed at the nearest birdhouse. "She would love these communal martin houses. Purple martins are such skilled fliers they can eat, drink, and even bathe on the wing. But pesticides are a serious threat. Their population is declining."

A purple martin poked its sleek head out of the house, chirped once, and hid back inside.

"I made all those birdhouses," said Mr. Smith.

"They're really nice." Loah nodded. "Thank you for helping protect the environment."

"You're welcome. Now, like I said." He pointed at the driveway. "And don't come back."

"PopPop, her mother had an accident," said Ellis. "In the *Arctic*."

"Ha! Right! Now *I'm* the Queen of England."

"It's true, PopPop!"

"Daddy." A voice from inside made them all turn. Behind the front window, Loah glimpsed a face pale and narrow as Ellis's. "Daddy, could you come here? I want to speak to you."

"In a minute."

"No. Now."

Mr. Smith rocked forward, flattening his feet on the ground. His scowl turned sulky. (Who knew scowls came in so many varieties?) He stomped up the wooden wheelchair ramp. Whoever had built it had done a good job, because it held firm and steady beneath his massive, stomping self.

"Is that your mother?" whispered Loah.

"Uh-huh. I still can't believe Zeke covered for me. I guess he knew I'd be safe with you."

Ellis slid her eyes toward the house, where her grandfather had left the front door standing open. Inside, Ellis's mother's voice rose.

"Squirrel says she's her friend. That means we help her."

"She's no—" tried PopPop.

"Besides, it's that child's mama. I don't care who she is or what she did, her mama's in trouble." When PopPop didn't answer, she said, "Daddy. Why are you still standing there? Get going!"

Mr. Smith appeared in the doorway. *Filled* the doorway, was more accurate. *Overflowed* it. He came back down the ramp, pulling a bandanna from his pocket and wiping his brow.

"You got dirt on your face," he said, holding it out to Loah.

Loah wiped her face and handed it back. "Thank you," she said.

He stuffed it back in his pocket and hurled a look at the house.

"The university." He spat on the ground, then trundled toward the truck.

"He's going to take us! He always does what Mama tells him to!" Ellis hugged Loah. "I'll be right back—I need to tell her thank you."

Ellis vaulted onto the porch and into the house. Through the window, Loah watched her bend over her mother. So much love shone in her face, Loah's eyes filled with tears. When her mother reached up to pull Ellis close, Loah felt a deep, deep ache for someone to hug her, hug her hard and close. But there was nobody to do that, so she threw her arms around Aquaman, who butted her and bounded away.

The pickup gave a roar. Evil-looking exhaust shot out the rear.

"You coming?" hollered Mr. Smith.

The truck's floor had a rusted-out hole wide enough to swallow a baby. Loah hunted for a seat belt. In vain. As Bully scrabbled into the rear seat, Ellis came running, but when she tried to climb in, Mr. Smith reached over Loah and slammed the door shut.

"Step away from the vehicle."

"PopPop! Please!"

"You heard me." He shifted gears, and the truck lurched forward.

CHAPTER TWENTY-SIX

Mr. Smith was so big, his head grazed the truck ceiling. He looked at Loah only once, a look that made her shrink against the door. She dug her fingers into a slit in the seat cushion as the truck shimmied and shook over the hill and onto the road.

The phrase *speed limit* wasn't part of Mr. Smith's vocabulary. When Loah looked down, she was horrified to see the road spinning just beneath her feet. She jerked her chin up in time to watch a woodchuck waddle into the road. She clapped her hands over her eyes and heard Mr. Smith swear as the truck swerved.

Bully rested his head on her shoulder and breathed swampy dog-breath on her cheek. The truck jolted and jounced, and she could feel her vital organs being shaken loose. She wasn't at all sure they were headed the right direction but was too afraid to speak.

"My daughter loves birds," Mr. Smith said, startling her. "Since she had the accident, she spends a lot of time watching them."

"I . . . I know. Ell . . . Little Squirrel told me."

"What else she tell you?"

"Oh. Umm. Not too much."

Mr. Smith nodded as if that was the right answer.

The sign for the university miraculously appeared. Mr. Smith asked what building it was and pulled into the nearest parking lot. Loah jumped out.

"Thank you very much, Mr. Smith. I really appreciate it." She wanted to ask him to tell Ellis she'd come by as soon as she could, but that would be pushing her luck. She shut the truck door and, with a small wave, started across the parking lot. Who knew how she'd get back? She couldn't worry about that now.

The campus had the feel of an abandoned city. The walkways were deserted. Faded flyers fluttered in the breeze. Through the windows she could see empty desks and blank whiteboards. From the distance came the faint sound of cheering: *You can do it, You can do it, You can do it, Yay!* Loah wondered if she was hallucinating. By now it seemed entirely possible.

Mama's building had bulletin boards with notices for fellowships and trips to exotic places Loah would never dream of going. The hall was lined with specimen cases displaying the bleached skeletons of birds and mammals. Loah's shoes squeaked on the linoleum floor. A workman stood on a ladder, installing a new light, but otherwise the building appeared empty. Riding with Mr. Smith had been so distracting, Loah's panic about her mother had quieted down, but now it surged back. What if she couldn't find anyone to help? She didn't have a Plan B.

The door to the Department of Mammalogy and Ornithology stood open. Across the empty reception area, through the door to an inner office, she spied Dr. Whitaker at a desk as messy as Dr. Londonderry's. Possibly messier. He was a handsome, dark-skinned man with a clean-shaven head and round glasses. When she stood in his doorway, he pushed those glasses up his nose with one finger, then folded his hands atop a teetering stack of papers.

"Good afternoon. Are you here to enroll?"

Though Loah had met him once or twice, she could tell he didn't remember her. (Not many people did.) He smiled pleasantly, if a little impatiently. The wall behind him was covered with framed certificates and photos of beautiful birds.

"I'm afraid you'll need to come back in a few years," he said.

"That's not why I'm here."

"That was supposed to be a joke. Are you looking for the cheerleading camp? It's in the fitness center, I think. Now you need to excuse me. This is my first day at my desk after being out of the country, and I have a lot to do."

He turned back to his work. Loah was dismissed.

"Actually . . . ," she said. He didn't look up, but she blundered on. "I'm here about Dr. Anastasia Londonderry."

"Ana? Not here, I'm afraid."

"I know." Loah began to feel a little dizzy. "That's what I want to tell you. Unless you already know. But I'm guessing you don't, since you've been away and since she didn't exactly want you to know what she was doing."

Dr. Whitaker possessed what people call *presence*. Never for a minute did you doubt who was in command of the conversation. When he looked up now, Loah had to steady herself against the doorframe.

"Who—? Hold on." He peered over the top of his glasses. "You're her daughter, aren't you?" When Loah nodded, he gestured at the chairs in front of the desk. "Sit down. You look like you need to sit down."

Loah slid into a chair so deep, her feet didn't touch the floor. Dr. Whitaker steepled his hands.

"Remind me of your name, please." His look was the kind that can make a person forget her own name. She gripped the arms of the chair.

"Loah."

"Loah. Yes. Of course." He smiled, leaning forward. "And you're here without your mother because . . . ?"

"Because she's still in the field."

Dr. Whitaker cupped his ear as if certain he'd heard wrong. His glasses slid back down his nose.

"She was due back over a week ago."

"I know. She's been gone sixty-eight days now."

He sat back. He blinked as if he still didn't comprehend, then began to tap on his laptop.

"I've received notes from the team, but I haven't had the chance yet to read them. Let me understand this. You're saying Dr. Londonderry continued the expedition without authorization?"

Did he have to make it sound so terrible?

"She's still there."

"There? Where is *there*?"

How did her mother have the courage to argue with him? Somehow, Loah managed to recite the GPS coordinates she'd memorized.

"That's the last place I know she was for sure. She's moved closer to the western coast since then. She heard a loah bird and so of course she—"

"She's gone rogue." He threw up his hands, sending a snowdrift of papers onto the floor. "Of all the pig-headed, unprofessional—"

"Dr. Whitaker, my mother is in trouble!"

He stood, got a cup of water from the cooler in the outer office, handed it to her, and sat back down.

"Tell me everything from the very beginning," he said.

The last thing Loah wanted to do was to recite the whole story all over again, but Dr. Whitaker was the sort of person who demanded an orderly, logical sequence. Usually, Loah was that sort of person, too, but now she wanted action. Still, she obediently drank some water, set the cup down, and did her best, beginning with the first call from her mother up until the one she'd received a few hours before. Dr. Whitaker pushed at his glasses. Shouldn't a man so important own glasses that fit? He squinted as if Loah were a rare species he was having trouble identifying. When she was finished, he leaned forward again, sending more papers sliding off the desk. Something about that desk gave Loah hope. For all their differences, her mother and Dr. Whitaker were both messy. Maybe they had more in common than she thought.

"Loah." Dr. Whitaker chose his next words carefully. "Loah Londonderry, your mother is a fine scientist. One of the best I've ever known. We definitely have our differences, but I respect and admire her. She is passionate. Most of us begin our careers brimming with passion, but the work can take it out of you. We're up against great odds these days. Some of us are running low on hope for the planet, but not Ana."

Loah's own hopes rose higher yet. Dr. Whitaker's gaze was intense as high-powered binoculars, but she did her best to look straight back.

"Furthermore..." His glasses were in danger of slipping off his nose, yet he didn't seem to notice. "She knows the ins and outs of the tundra as well as anyone possibly can."

It was all true. Under Dr. Whitaker's steely stare, Loah began to crumple. What if she was making a huge mistake? What if her mother had been in trouble but already gotten out of it, the way she always did? And if she really was in serious trouble, why would she call Loah? Why wouldn't she have called an expert, a team member, someone who'd know exactly what to do and how to do it, instead of Loah, who was as powerless as a small, wheezy, possibly extinct bird?

"I'm going to call her myself," Dr. Whitaker said.

Loah listened as her mother's phone rang once, then went dead.

Dr. Whitaker stared at the ceiling for a long moment, then once again tapped the keys of his laptop. Behind his glasses, his eyes grew troubled.

"I don't like these weather reports." He sat back. "All right, Loah. Now you've got me worried, too." He pressed his palms together and touched his fingertips to his nose.

Moments passed. Loah stared at the photos on the wall behind him. They showed beautiful, brilliantly colored birds, the kinds of birds that inspire people to write poetry and songs, not humble ones like the loah. At last Dr. Whitaker spoke.

"You need to understand, initiating a search mission in the Arctic is highly expensive and possibly dangerous. It's the absolute last thing your mother would want us to undertake on her account, unless it was absolutely necessary. It'd be irresponsible of me to set this in motion unless I'm one hundred percent sure of what you're telling me." His voice softened. "Loah, I know how worried you are. But I want you to think a moment longer."

Think. Loah tried. One of the photos showed a clutch of sp
led eggs. They were tucked into a nest woven of grasses and m
The egg—it was so sturdy and so fragile at the same time.
perfect construction, Loah heard her mother say. She felt her moth
finger stroke her curls as she added, *And it's made to be broken.*

Were those speckled eggs about to hatch? Had the chick
inside grown so big their egg teeth touched the shell? Did the
understand they no longer fit in their small, familiar world and the
time had come to crack it open?

She stood up so quickly, she sent more papers flying off the desk.

"I'm sure. You have to look for her. Right away. Please."

He held her eyes another moment, then waved at the outer
office. "Have a seat there."

Loah didn't move. "You'll search for her?"

"If it's warranted, we—"

"You'll do everything possible?"

"Yes, Loah."

"You'll make sure they keep looking till they find her? They
can find her, can't they?"

Dr. Whitaker stood up. "You're her daughter all right," he said,
and it almost sounded like a compliment. He ushered her to his
door. "Go have a seat."

In the outer office, Loah bit the insides of her cheeks. She tugged
on her earlobes. She clasped and unclasped her hands. She strained
to hear his deep voice, the rapid clicks of his keyboard. Dr. Anastasia Londonderry had registered her trip with the search-and-rescue
team in Talaallit, she heard. They reported that she had not acti-
vated her personal locator beacon.

"It's possible she couldn't," Loah heard him say.

153

The window was open. From the distance came the cheers of the cheerleading camp, and there, just outside the window, the echoing *cheer cheer* of a northern cardinal. Somewhere a dog began to bark.

And bark. And bark.

Dr. Whitaker came out of his office. His glasses were on top of his head. In spite of everything her mother had said about him, and everything he had said about her mother, Loah trusted him.

"Things are under way," he said.

He didn't say, *Don't worry* or *Everything will be fine.* Which made her trust him even more.

"Thank you," she said.

"Question: What are you doing here by yourself? Who's taking care of you?"

"Who wants to know?"

Mr. Smith loomed in the doorway. He was as sweaty as if he'd crossed a vast desert or plain and wasn't sure where he'd ended up. *I am in unexplored territory,* said his scowl.

"You find her mama yet?"

Dr. Whitaker cleared his throat. He resettled his glasses on his nose.

"Dr. Whitaker, this is Mr. Smith," said Loah. "Mr. Smith, this is Dr. Whitaker."

Dr. Whitaker held out his hand, which Mr. Smith ignored. "You find her?" he repeated.

"We're working on it." Dr. Whitaker said. "The tundra is vast and not exactly hospitable to humans." Dr. Whitaker's phone began to ring, and he retreated to his office.

Mr. Smith pulled out his bandanna and mopped his brow. Here in the office, Loah was aware of his sharp, not to say stinky, odor.

"Loah," called Dr. Whitaker. "Could you come here?" When she stepped inside his office, he closed the door, looking concerned. "Who is this fellow? He doesn't exactly seem like . . . If you're even the slightest bit afraid of him, tell me right now."

"He's my best friend's grandfather."

"He's trustworthy? I don't need to worry about him? You're sure?"

Loah (still) never lied unless she had to. She hesitated. Mr. Smith could have driven off and left her here—in fact, she'd been sure he would. Instead, he'd waited for her. Not only that, he'd come to make sure that she was all right and that these useless, fat-headed university people were helping her find her mother.

"I'm sure," she told Dr. Whitaker for the second time.

Dr. Whitaker waited another beat, then nodded. "I'm coming to trust your judgment." He exhaled. "Will he drive you home?"

"I can't go home! I need to stay here and help!"

"You've already helped. Thank God you came in. And thank God you convinced me. I'm not an easy person to convince, as your mother would testify." The phone began to ring again. His computer pinged. "We're hoping for the best, but this could be a long, unpleasant wait. You'll be better off at home."

"I'm steady in a crisis. Just ask Miss Rinker."

"Who?"

"Please. Please don't make me go."

He picked up the phone. "Whit here. Could you hold a moment?" Pressing the phone to his chest, he waited for Loah to leave, and when she didn't, he pursed his lips.

"You know, I remember when you were born. It was soon after the last time a loah—that ghost bird—was reported. Your mother brought you in to show you off, and when she told us your name, it was so perfect, we all started cheering. I think we scared you, though. You started bawling. And then you got a killer case of hiccups."

"I still do that."

"She talks about you all the time, you know."

She does? Loah thought. She wanted to ask what her mother said, but the computer pinged again and Dr. Whitaker steered her toward the door.

"I'm sorry she went off alone," he said. "Very sorry. But we will find her. I promise you that. As soon as we know anything, I'll tell you. Anything—I promise. Now I've got to take this call."

He opened the door. Mr. Smith stood right outside it.

CHAPTER TWENTY-SEVEN

This time, the ride back felt much shorter than the ride there.

When the truck pulled up in front of Loah's house, Bully commenced barking. It was impossible to tell if he sensed danger or was barking for no reason whatsoever. Mr. Smith hadn't said a word the whole way, and no sooner did Loah's feet hit the ground than he pulled away in a cloud of evil exhaust.

Then backed up.

"Little Squirrel is hardheaded. She gets that from me."

"Oh."

"If she says you're her friend, count on it."

"Well, I'm her friend, too."

He peered at the house, all but swallowed up by the trees. "You going to be all right here by yourself?"

"Yes."

His scowl was dubious.

"You can stay with us. Squirrel and her mother would like that."

"Thanks, Mr. Smith. But I'm always happiest when I'm home."

He nodded as if that was the right answer. Bully barked, and they drove away.

Miss Rinker had left many messages. Theo, she said, continued to recover. The doctors insisted on keeping her, though she kept telling them she was perfectly fine. Why on earth didn't Loah call her?

When Loah did, a nurse answered.

"She's asleep," he said in a low voice. "Do you want me to wake her?"

"No thank you. Just tell her Loah called."

Loah's goldfish blew a delicate stream of silvery bubbles. It flicked its lovely, translucent tail. Had the fish always been so beautiful, or had living here made it shine this bright? Loah and the fish kept each other company as she ate cold mashed potatoes and it nibbled fish flakes. She carefully carried the bowl up to her room, where she set it on the night table beside the photo of her and her mother. Kneeling on her bed, she spoke to the loah bird.

"If you're there—if you managed to survive and I really hope you did—if you're there and you see her, could you...could you maybe...maybe somehow watch over her? Since I can't?"

The bird would not meet her eye.

The night was long.

Very long.

The next morning, Loah put on her CREW poncho for comfort, then sat in her mother's desk chair. She was staring at the phone when tires crunched the gravel drive. She raced along the hall and out the back door, forgetting the rotting last step, which collapsed once and for all and so completely, the earth itself seemed to give way beneath her feet. The poncho made a completely ineffective parachute.

"Loah Londonderry?" A woman bustled toward her. Her hair was patchy—gray, white, and black. If she'd been a cat, she'd have been a plump tabby. "Are you all right, hon?"

"Did Dr. Whitaker send you? Did they find my mother?"

The woman had soulful green eyes. Their edges crimped with sadness.

"Oh dear," she said. "So she *is* missing." She helped Loah up, then opened her purse. "Don't worry, hon. I'm here to help." She extracted a small card and handed it to Loah: *Margaret Murphy, MSW, Child Protection Services.*

Protection? From what?

"What is that you're wearing, hon? Don't you have proper clothing?"

"This is my . . ." How to explain Miss Rinker's bargain poncho to a stranger? "Never mind. If you're not here about my mother, then—"

"But I am. My office has received reports of lack of adult supervision." Ms. Murphy's voice was soothing, almost apologetic. "I'm here to see what's what."

As if on cue, Inspector Kipper's car pulled into the driveway. He strode purposefully toward them, wearing the solemn, important look of an adult who's certain that he knows better than you do, and that one day you'll be deeply grateful for his wisdom.

Loah considered ducking inside and locking the doors, but what good would that do? Clearly, the inspector was not giving up. This time he'd brought reinforcements.

"Hello, Margaret," said Inspector Kipper. "Thank you for coming."

"We were just getting acquainted." Ms. Murphy smiled

brightly at Loah, who edged away backward. "We were discussing her missing mother."

Loah wanted to say her mother wasn't missing, but—at the risk of being awfully repetitive—she hated to lie. As it happened, there was no time to speak anyway, because just then a harsh scraping sound made them all look up. No! Not now! Ms. Murphy gasped and gripped Loah's arm as a slate tobogganed off the roof and smashed into the ground.

"Good heavens." Ms. Murphy gasped. "I see what you mean, Wayne."

Loah attempted to retrieve her arm, but Ms. Murphy held fast.

"Poor thing. Have you eaten lately? Are you hungry?" She fumbled one-handed in her purse.

Though there was no breeze, the trees began to stir. Feathery rustles, flickery whispers. Bright tufts and dark crowns, tilting and twisting. And then, out of nowhere, as if the air had conjured it— the vulture. Its thick talons clicked against the slates. Mrs. Murphy, extracting a cereal bar from her purse, gave a second, even bigger, gasp. The purse fell from her hand.

"Is that a buzzard?"

"Vicious bird of prey," said Inspector Kipper. "Quite possibly diseased."

Loah picked up the purse and handed it back. "Vultures only eat carrion," she said, "which is meat that's already dead."

"Ooh." Ms. Murphy dropped the purse again.

Like a snake with wings, the vulture hissed. Its stony eyes bored into Loah, trying to tell her something she tried to understand. *Stand your ground.* Or was it *Beware?* Up in the trees, deep in the bushes, tucked in the ivy, more birds gathered.

"You can see the situation, Margaret," said the inspector.

"Please," said Loah. "You don't understand."

"It's not your fault, hon," said Ms. Murphy in that infuriatingly soothing voice. She took Loah's arm again. "You've done nothing wrong."

"I know that!" cried Loah.

Ms. Murphy gasped her third gasp as a car hairpinned into the driveway. Brakes screeched, gravel flew, and the car's front bumper crunched into the rear bumper of Inspector Kipper's official vehicle.

"Hey!" he cried.

It was Loah's turn to gasp. "You're here!" she said.

The feather on Miss Rinker's hat quivered as she climbed out of the car and mashed Loah to her cactus-y chest.

"Are you all right? Why didn't you answer the phone? I was so worried. Tell me you're all right, Loah Londonderry!"

"Now," said Loah. "Now I am."

Miss Rinker's head swiveled—from Loah to Inspector Kipper to Ms. Murphy then back to Loah. At that moment, something that Loah had never witnessed in eleven and a half years happened.

Miss Rinker went speechless.

Inspector Kipper, however, was never at a loss for words. Unfortunately.

"Ma'am? Hello. Can I ask who you might be?"

She blinked at him. "I know who I am, not who I might be. Who *you* are is the question."

"Inspector Wayne J. Kipper, housing department." He removed his red cap, revealing his bald spot and ring of dented hair. "And this is Margaret Murphy from child protection services. May I ask your relationship to this property and to this child?"

"Relationship? I...We...This is the beloved home of me and my brother, and this..." She turned to face Loah, who realized with a jolt that they had somehow become the same height. Miss Rinker's eyes narrowed. She believed in the truth, even when it hurt. Especially when it hurt. But apparently she also believed in deciding for herself what the truth was. "This is our one and only family."

Have you ever wished you could stop time? Pause it so you could enjoy something a little bit longer? If so, you know how Loah felt just then.

"Your family calls you Miss Rinker?" said the investigator.

"I'll thank you to do the same," said Miss Rinker.

"Miss Rinker. It's against the law to go off and leave a minor alone under any circumstances. And these circumstances—"

"Go off?" Miss Rinker rocked backward as if struck a blow. "Whatever do you mean?"

Swift and stealthy as arrows, still more birds gathered. The vulture hopped off the roof and into the gutter. This close, it was even uglier, but ugliness no longer seemed like the main thing about it. Maybe this was because Mr. Smith, in his own way, had been so kind to her, or because Miss Rinker, who never hugged, had hugged her as if her life depended on it, or maybe it was because Loah was not the girl she used to be, but whatever the cause, she saw the vulture differently now. Something her mother had told her about vultures whispered in the back of her mind. . . .

"In point of fact, every time I've been here Loah has been alone, in a structure that does not meet our municipality's standards of housing."

A jay screeched, and the inspector's shoulders rose around his ears. Yet he stood his ground. Say what you will about him, Inspector Kipper believed in his mission. He explained that the tower (would he never learn?) was a menace, the trees a disaster in the making, the rotting step and crumbling roof serious hazards, and there were predatory and potentially disease-ridden creatures on the premises. He pointed at the vulture.

"Numerous notices have been ignored. Meanwhile, Loah Londonberry, a nice little girl though she needs some new friends, seems to have been abandoned."

By now Miss Rinker had grown deathly pale. With all she'd been through in the last several days, with all she'd been through since she was a child, you'd think she could easily stand up to a pipsqueak like Inspector Kipper. Yet his accusations seemed to knock her off her feet. Her lips worked soundlessly. She tottered. Her hand went to her heart, and she began to tremble so hard she had to lean against Loah.

Who felt anger blaze up inside her. No—not anger. Make that *fury*. Any anger she'd felt in the past was a campfire compared to this. This was a wildfire. She put her arm around Miss Rinker. Her bones like toothpicks. Her chin sharp as an ax.

"Miss Rinker knows what it's like to be abandoned. She knows how terrible it is, and she'd never let it happen to me. She and her brother are homebodies, just like me, and when my mother's not here, Miss Rinker and Theo are."

Loah pulled up a lawn chair and helped Miss Rinker into it. Maybe you're thinking that by this point, Loah had used up her anger, which, like courage, she had in only limited supply. But it was actually getting stronger.

"My mother, Dr. Anastasia London*derry*, is dedicated to saving birds and their habitats. You say you care about homes, Inspector Kipper. Well, dozens and dozens and *dozens* of species of birds, mammals, fish, insects, and plants are losing theirs even as we speak! Do you even care?"

Something was happening overhead. The birds seemed to be conferring with one another, though that was impossible. Robins never speak to sparrows, and cardinals don't communicate with nuthatches. But twitters and warbles flew back and forth, sharing some common language understood by every mysterious bird brain. The vulture shifted on its clumsy feet, never taking its eyes off Loah.

"I'm sorry she ignored your inspection notices. She didn't mean to break the law. It's just . . . Sometimes she gets so caught up in her work, that other things, she forgets . . ."

Loah's voice began to fold up. Do not do not do not. Do. Not. Cry.

"My mother will be home soon," she managed to say. "And when she is . . . when she gets home again . . ."

What if she didn't?

"Oh, hon." Ms. Murphy's soulful green eyes glittered with tears. "You love your mother very much, and I'm sure she loves you just the same. How could she help it?" She turned to Miss Rinker. "My own mother died when I was young. I was raised by my grandmother, and I owe her everything. She'd have loved your hat, by the way. Listen, Miss Brinker. I'll have to do a follow-up assessment, but for now I'm going to leave Loah under your supervision. You two take good care of each other, okay?"

Miss Rinker managed a nod.

Ms. Murphy gave Loah the cereal bar, got in her car, and drove away. Inspector Kipper, however—surprise, surprise—was not satisfied.

"It's impossible to get anything straight around this place." His face was edging toward a shade of red that matched his cap. "But I'll tell you this. Dr. London*derry* is in violation of the law. She's putting this property at risk. Soon it'll be out of my hands."

The vulture made a new sound, one Loah had never heard. Its throat began to wrinkle in a weird way, but the inspector, riffling through his papers, didn't notice.

"Legal proceedings will proceed," he said.

A house sparrow—could it be the same one she'd begged not to die?—landed at Loah's feet. It took a few hops, looking over its shoulder. *Follow me.* It hopped farther away into the trees. *Come on.*

Loah followed. Meanwhile, the vulture tilted side to side, eyes slitted, red throat convulsing. What was it doing? The sparrow threw another look over its feathered shoulder. *Look out.*

That was the moment that Loah remembered what her mother had told her about vulture defense mechanisms.

"Inspector Kipper," she said, "you should step back."

He ignored her, continuing to hunt through his papers. The vulture's neck pulsed. It throbbed.

"Inspector Kipper!"

Annoyed, he raised his face, just as the vulture opened its beak and shot out a geyser of the most repulsive-smelling vomit imaginable. (If you are squeamish, don't even try to imagine it.) The puke spewed in a great arc that hung in the air for a brief, grotesque moment before splattering his face, cap, and shoulders.

The inspector was too stunned to move. Which made him the perfect target for the vulture to do it again.

Was that a decapitated mouse head on his cap? Loah didn't mean to laugh. She really didn't.

We all have our limits. Being showered in reeking vomit containing partly digested chunks of rodent was Inspector Kipper's, at least for today. Hurling his ruined cap to the ground, he said something unrepeatable. Puke-spotted pages fell from his folder as he snapped it shut.

He climbed into his official vehicle, whose bumper was dented and whose upholstery was going to stink to high heaven for a long time, but Miss Rinker's car had him boxed in. As he tried to maneuver out, several birds took the opportunity to unleash their own opinions on his windshield.

When he was finally gone, Loah looked up at the roof, wanting to thank the vulture, but it had vanished.

"Loah." Miss Rinker's voice was a whisper. "Is Dr. Londonderry all right?"

Loah pulled a chair close to hers. As she explained, Miss Rinker clutched at her cactus-y sweater. Her lip drew back, showing her ill-fitting dentures. By the time Loah finished, Miss Rinker's eyes were blurry with tears.

"I should have been here for you," she whispered. "I'm sorry."

There had been many times—more times than she could count—when Loah had wished to hear those words from Miss Rinker. Now was not one of those times.

"I kept busy. And I tried not to be afraid. Those are things you taught me, Miss Rinker."

Miss Rinker took her hand. Mama said all living creatures depended on one another in ways big and small, ways they knew and ways they never guessed at, and she was right. Mama! Loah's eyes filled with tears. Where was she? Loah lifted her face, and her breath caught as, all at once, the birds exploded out of the trees.

A quarrel of sparrows. A confusion of warblers. A murmuration of starlings, a charm of finches, a radiance of cardinals! Swooping down, they spun the world into wings and beaks, bright feathers and piercing eyes. The air around Loah and Miss Rinker swirled. The light shattered into dazzling bits. Miss Rinker and Loah held tight to each other as the birds looped this way and that, weaving a wild, heart-stopping blanket, a nest of air and song. It was frightening and wonderful beyond words, and Loah, trembling, felt as if her mother were right here with her. In the beat of their wings, between the trills and calls, she could hear Mama whisper, *A place brimming with surprise and wonder and beauty for the finding . . .*

The gravel in the driveway crunched, and the birds whirled up and out of sight so quickly that Loah might have thought she'd imagined it, except for Miss Rinker's hand clutching hers and the singly perfect, deep blue feather drifting down to settle in her lap as Dr. Whitaker climbed out of his car and slowly, solemnly came toward them.

"We found her," he said.

CHAPTER TWENTY-EIGHT

The blue feather lay on the kitchen table as Dr. Whitaker took off his glasses and ran a hand over his eyes. He'd already outlined what had happened to Dr. Londonderry. Now, choosing each word carefully, he was about to fill in the details when the door banged open and Ellis burst into the room.

"Loah!" Her cheeks were pink, her hair windblown. Seeing them sitting there, she froze. "Oh," she whispered. "Oh."

Loah jumped up and led her to the table.

"This is my friend Ellis Smith. Ellis, this is Miss Rinker and this is Dr. Whitaker."

Miss Rinker gave the barest nod. Dr. Whitaker carefully hooked his glasses over his ears. He folded his hands on the table, cleared his throat, and continued.

The conditions Dr. Londonderry had described earlier had only gotten worse. Travel had been treacherous at best. She was down to her last bit of food and relying on marsh water she purified. Turning back was the only sensible decision. Dr. Whitaker paused. A muscle in his cheek twitched.

"She pressed on."

Miss Rinker inched her chair closer to Loah's.

Dr. Londonderry's Jeep must have hit a collapsed pingo or a crater. The permafrost was badly heaved in every direction. The Jeep rolled over, skidded on its side, and came to a stop against some boulders. The rescue team who found her reported that it had a broken axle.

Dr. Whitaker pulled a sigh from his very depths.

"She was dehydrated and in shock with a badly broken arm. The first thing she said to the crew was, *Where is Loah?* When they said they hadn't seen the bird, she said, *No! My girl. Where is my girl?* She was convinced you were there with her."

Miss Rinker slid an arm around Loah.

So did Ellis.

In its bowl, the fish hid behind its plant.

They helicoptered her out. By the time they reached the hospital, they had her hydrated. Doctors pieced her arm back together with pins and screws, a process Loah didn't want to think about. Never, ever would she be a doctor, but she would be eternally grateful to anyone who was.

"So?" whispered Ellis. "She . . ."

"She was astonishingly lucky," Dr. Whitaker said. "Her injuries could have been much worse. And if they hadn't found her when they did . . ." He looked at the ceiling, then back at Loah. "You and the rescue team saved her life."

Ellis flung herself out of her chair. "You did it!" she cried, hugging Loah.

"She did," said Dr. Whitaker. "You're a hero, Loah Londonderry."

No. Being a hero meant you were courageous, even fearless, two things Loah hoped never to need to be again. She'd had more than enough of adventure and peril.

She opened her mouth to say so, but Miss Rinker summoned all her old, indomitable force to command, "Do not argue."

"Ana was only able to talk for a few minutes," Dr. Whitaker said. "She listened to my tirade about how foolish, pigheaded, and completely irresponsible she'd been, and she completely agreed. Then immediately tried to convince me to mount a return expedition."

"She wouldn't!" Miss Rinker bared her dentures.

"I don't see it happening," said Dr. Whitaker. "Ana never got a photo. No recording, no concrete evidence. Reactions will range from skeptical to dismissive." He reached for a MERRY CHRISTMAS napkin and dabbed his eyes. "She'll call you later today, Loah. It'll be a while before she's stable enough to travel, though if it were up to her, she'd be on a plane to you right now."

He pushed back his chair and stood up. He looked tired, tired to the bone. He'd kept his promise to find her mother, no matter what it took, and Loah would have hugged him if she dared. He was so solid, so reasonable, so trustworthy, and she thought how nice it would be to have a parent like that. A parent right out of *One and Only Family.*

"Thank you," she said. "Thank you from the bottom of my heart."

"Thank *you.* If anything had happened to her . . . well." He put a hand on her shoulder, crinkling the poncho she still wore. "You might not believe me, but I wish she'd gotten proof your bird was still out there."

"Dr. Whitaker, you told me yourself, she's one of the best scientists you've ever known. Do you really think she made a mistake?"

He gave a small, weary smile.

"Let's just get her home safe," he said. "Then she and I can talk."

Loah walked him down the corridor, across the entry hall and under the stag-head chandelier. At the door he stopped.

"I'm not sure about the bird," he said, "but you, Loah Londonderry. You are a rare find." He shook her hand, then stepped outside, where a goldfinch did a lovely loop-de-loop in the green summer air.

"Mama." Loah sat in Theo's lounger, phone clasped tight.

"Sweetie."

"How do you feel?"

"Foolish. And very, very sorry. Sweetheart! Whit told me what you did. What you had to go through! I never should have stayed, but I had to. Oh, sweetie, that's not much of an apology, is it? It was a chance I had to take, but I wish I never . . . I'm sorry—I'm still not making sense."

"Mama? Do you think the loah will be all right? Do you think her eggs will survive?" When her mother didn't answer, Loah said, "She managed all this time on her own. She's smart and strong. I don't know if birds can be brave, but if they can, she is."

"Oh, sweetie." Her mother began to cry. "So are you! All those things."

"I think she's out there. And if she has chicks . . . I think they're all going to be fine."

Usually it was Theo who made sure Loah went to bed on time, who smuggled her gummy worms or whistled her a good-night tune, then sat for a while, listening to the screech owl's spooky lullaby.

Things were different tonight. Tonight it was Miss Rinker, and instead of the owl, another bird called outside the window. The northern mockingbird knows hundreds of songs, most borrowed from other birds, and it can sing for hours, mixing whistles and trills, caws and chirps and coos, without ever repeating itself. Tonight the mockingbird serenaded them as Miss Rinker supervised Loah doing her ocular exercises, taking her shower, and combing every last tangle from her curls. It was Miss Rinker who neatened the bedcovers, straightened the picture of the Loah bird, wiped smudges from the side of the fishbowl, all the while muttering darkly about whether that bird outside would ever stop its racket.

When at last Loah was in bed, Miss Rinker folded her pipe-cleaner arms. By now she'd mostly recovered from the shock of the day, and looked like her old self. Loah was sure she'd find something to lecture about. It might sound peculiar to you, if you dislike being scolded and lectured—and who doesn't?—but the fact was that Loah almost looked forward to it. Remember how much she loved the familiar and predictable. A Miss Rinker scolding would be immensely comforting.

The old woman's eyes shone in a way that made Loah think she looked forward to the lecture, too. But Miss Rinker, it turned out, was not the same person she'd been. She bared her dentures. Her bushy eyebrows drew together.

"You've been on an expedition," she announced.

Poor Miss Rinker! The day must have truly addled her.

"No," said Loah gently. "That would be my mother."

"Expeditions come in every size and shape. You can be an explorer without ever leaving home."

"But—"

"Do not argue. You will never win."

Miss Rinker dropped a papery kiss on Loah's forehead, switched off the light, and marched away.

What could Miss Rinker mean? The deep blue feather the birds had given her lay on the bedside table, and Loah took it in her fingers. Maybe, maybe if you looked at things a certain way, every life was a kind of expedition. Going forward, one step after another. Even when you thought you knew where you were headed, there'd be a surprise, sometimes for better and sometimes for worse. You might discover something wonderful, something that had been there all along, just waiting for you to find it. Something like a friend. Or how good you were at being a friend. Or how hard you'd fight to save the places and people you loved.

She touched the feather to her cheek. But sometimes, many times, the expedition would be hard. You'd discover things you'd rather not. Maybe you'd discover that, though your mother loved you, she loved the natural world just as much. Maybe, sometimes, she loved it even more than she loved you. To fight for it, to protect it, she'd leave you. Again and again, her work would pull her away from you.

The mockingbird sang. Loah closed her eyes.

Mama had to be Mama, and Loah had to be Loah. Only not exactly the Loah she used to be. Mama would go away, and she would stay home, and that would never be easy, but it would be different now. Loah drew a breath and felt it fill her. She stretched her legs and knew they'd grown. Always, always, she would want Mama to come home, but it would be a different kind of wanting. Not the helpless kind. Because Loah wasn't helpless, not anymore.

Opening her eyes for a moment, she saw a single moonbeam, white as a snow goose feather, tumble over the lovely dark wall of trees. The world was big and the world was small and that was the mystery of it. The mystery and the wonder and . . .

The mockingbird sang Loah off to sleep.

CHAPTER TWENTY-NINE

Along the hallway with its peeling wallpaper, down the staircase with its faded carpet of cabbage roses, across the entry hall with its stag-head chandelier, along another dim corridor, and into the kitchen with its checkered black-and-white tile floor...

On the table sat a big cake whose icing spelled out HAPPY 33RD ANNIVERSARY MARY AND... The rest of the letters were smooshed into oblivion. The cake had been on discount at the bakery, and Miss Rinker, even today, could not resist a bargain.

She'd bought it on her way home from the rehab center, where Theo was making steady progress. He'd be home within the week. Loah had been to see him every day, bringing him gummy worms and reading to him from a new book the librarian with the sparkly purple glasses had given her, a biography of Nellie Bly (real name: Elizabeth Cochrane Seaman), who had traveled by steamship and train around the world in seventy-two days (much faster than Magellan) and lived to tell.

Loah and Theo agreed that coming home safe and sound was Nellie Bly's greatest accomplishment.

And speaking of coming home...

At this very moment, Dr. Whitaker was at the airport picking up Loah's mother.

"Just a little while, Crew," she told her goldfish.

It was Zeke who'd finally named it. He kept following Ellis here, though she threatened to remove his head and spit down his neck. When Miss Rinker gave him a new poncho to replace the filthy yellow fringe his old one had become, he thanked her as if she'd given him a magic wand. When he'd said they should name the fish Crew, it blew a jubilant stream of bubbles. *Yes.*

Ellis brought Loah homemade cookies, bottles of homemade grape juice, and lumps of homemade goat cheese (these Loah carefully placed in the very back of the refrigerator). As soon as things calmed down enough, Loah was going to the hollow to choose a kitten from the newest litter in the barn. She couldn't bring it home, of course, but it would be hers, Ellis promised. Loah had already chosen *its* name.

Nestle.

A few days ago, Mr. Smith had given Ellis a ride here. Pulling into the driveway, he'd watched Loah hop down the back steps, and scowled. Later, when he returned, the bed of the pickup held tools and fresh boards, and soon there was a new bottom step. PopPop, it turned out, knew how to make more than birdhouses. He'd built Ellis's mother's wheelchair ramp, the many sheds, the goats' fence. Watching him wield sharp tools had made Loah's heart quake a little, but it had also given her an idea.

Now as she hurried down the steps, all of them freshly painted, she hoped her mother would approve when she found out Loah had hired Mr. Smith. He'd be back soon to clean the gutters and replace the roof slates. Meanwhile, she'd called the number on Inspector Wayne J. Kipper's card and told him that repairs on the house had begun and he could come meet her mother next week. She could tell he didn't believe her. She could hardly wait till he saw for himself.

She strolled across the yard and sat on her swing. Overhead, the birds were fizzy with joy. The kind of joy that comes from knowing that the world will always brim with new wonder and surprise. Song stitched the air. Even the jay was trying to sing. Perched in the oak, black feather necklace gleaming on its brilliant white chest, it made soft clicks and clucks, instead of its usual awful screeches.

Bird brains are wired for joy. They know the world is a dangerous place, yet anytime they can forget it, they do.

A grunt. A hiss.

Loah looked up, and there was the vulture, hulking in its favorite spot next to the turret. It spread its raggedy wings and shifted its scaly feet. Loah almost laughed. There was no getting rid of it.

"You're back! Why?"

The vulture fixed her with its stony eyes. *I've been trying to tell you. If you weren't so dense, you'd have figured it out by now.*

So many strange, unpredictable things had happened lately, possibly more things than had happened in Loah's entire life, yet what came next was one of a kind. No, two of a kind. Because before her very eyes, the bird doubled. A second vulture, indistinguishable from the first, slipped out from inside the turret.

"What?" She rubbed her eyes. Slowly, then all at once, the truth dawned. "Wait. It was you? Making those noises? Scaring me like that? The two of you?" She rubbed her eyes again. "What? Three?"

A creature covered in fuzzy white feathers squeezed out next. A small shake, a hoarse peep, and it began toddling around looking immensely pleased with itself. A baby! A chick.

177

Followed by its sibling.

Squinting hard at the crooked turret, Loah saw the spot where the hunk of masonry had broken loose, but now she also saw, for the first time, a barely visible chink in the other side. The thumping. The hissing. The flashes of raw-meat red. All this time, it had been a volt of vultures! The turret with its broken windowpane and crumbling stone—all this time, it had been a home, birthing and sheltering a new family.

The chicks' faces were shaped like ebony hearts. Their pink feet were much too big for the rest of them. Puffing their chests, they hissed like fluffy teakettles. They flapped their useless, fledgling wings. Meanwhile, their parents hovered about, protective and proud.

No wonder the vulture had stood its ground and refused to leave. The vultures. This was their home.

Their home and hers. Never had Loah loved it more than at this moment.

The chicks toddled to the edge of the roof, peeked over, and scurried back in alarm. Loah burst out laughing. They weren't ready to leave the nest. Oh no, no way! They'd done the first hard work of pecking their way out of their shells, and next they'd learn to fly. But not yet. Not for a while. How would they know when it was time? How would they know their wings were ready? Mama would have the answer to that.

Tires crunched the gravel, and Loah spun around to see Dr. Whitaker's car. There was Mama, leaning out the passenger window, grinning and waving with her good arm. Loah had so much to ask Mama, and even more—so much more—to tell her.

Loah the homebody, Loah the explorer, flew to meet her.

AUTHOR'S NOTE

The loah bird doesn't actually exist, any more than Loah Londonderry does, though now that you've finished reading their story, I hope both will be as real and as dear to you as they are to me. (Note: In this book all Arctic places names are, likewise, fictional.)

While I made up the loah bird, the other facts in this book are all true. Birds are such astonishing creatures, I had no need to invent. Birds have owned the sky for over 150 million years. They inhabit every corner of our earth, from the most isolated wildernesses to the centers of the busiest cities. Travel to the coldest mountain peak or the hottest, driest desert, and birds will be there, laying their eggs, raising their young, lacing the air with their songs. It's a fact that the Arctic tern migrates from its Arctic breeding grounds to the Antarctic and back again each year, approximately twenty thousand miles. Equally amazing, the common swift can stay in nonstop flight for up to ten months. (How does it sleep? Another bird mystery.) It's true that the peregrine falcon, which has colonized many cities, can reach a speed of over two hundred miles an hour when diving for prey. (In a race, a cheetah would not stand a chance.) It's also a true and endearing fact that turkey vultures are very social birds that love to hang out with friends, though during mating season parent birds stick close to each other and the nest.

The birds in our own backyards and neighborhood green spaces may not seem as amazing, but look again. Watch a noisy, nosy blue jay hold a seed between its feet and crack it open with its powerful beak, or that little acrobat the hairy woodpecker whack a tree trunk in search of its insect supper. Listen to a northern mockingbird with

179

its hilarious medley of mimicked songs and sounds. In spring, keep an eye out for bits of the beautiful blue shell of the American robin. This egg has protected and nurtured a growing chick for weeks. Like all bird eggs, from the tiniest hummingbird's to the colossal ostrich's, it was the perfect size for its inhabitant. It was exactly the right shape for its nest. If you find pieces of it on the sidewalk or grass, you'll know it has done its job: it has given way to new life.

Unfortunately, while I didn't need to invent a single brilliant, lovable fact about birds, I also didn't need to invent their current plight. If you go to the website of the International Union for Conservation of Nature (www.iucn.org), which Loah mentions, you'll find its Red List of Endangered Species. You will not, of course, find the loah bird, but as of 2021 over thirty thousand species of birds, mammals, amphibians, and other creatures—about 27 percent of all assessed species—are listed as endangered. While it's a fact that climate change is affecting the Arctic at twice the rate of the rest of the globe, creatures and plants everywhere are suffering from its impact. In addition, as developers exhaust Earth's natural resources—for example, by mass deforestation—they often disrupt wildlife's food sources and shelters. Loah and her mother never even mention the impact that drilling for oil in the Arctic could have on its Native peoples' communities, as well as on animals like the polar bear, snow goose, and snowy owl.

"Hope is the thing with feathers," wrote the poet Emily Dickinson. Humans have long seen birds as symbols of hope, peace, beauty, and freedom. Far from giving up the fight to save them and their habitats, scientists and conservationists young and old are working with great urgency. We can all do our part. While few of us will go on expeditions like Dr. Londonderry's, all of us can, like Loah, nurture the places and people we love.

SELECTED BIBLIOGRAPHY

BOOKS

Attenborough, David. *The Life of Birds*. Princeton, NJ: Princeton University Press, 1998.

Schomp, Virginia. *24 Hours on the Tundra (A Day in an Ecosystem)*. New York: Cavendish Square Publishing, 2012.

Stemple, Heidi E. Y. *Counting Birds: The Idea That Helped Save Our Feathered Friends*. Illustrated by Clover Robin. Lake Forest, CA: Seagrass Press, 2018.

Thompson, Bill, III. *The Young Birder's Guide to Birds of North America*. Peterson Field Guides. Boston: Houghton Mifflin Harcourt, 2012.

FILMS

Attenborough, David. *The Life of Birds*. Ten-part BBC/PBS series. 1998.

Collardy, Samuel. *Arctic Boyhood*. A short documentary about an eight-year-old boy living in the village of Tiniteqilaaq, Greenland, 1998. www.youtube.com/watch?v=5_vBbw0FrGs.

WEBSITES

eBird. A project of the Cornell Lab of Ornithology with a mobile app
that lets you track your own sightings and compare with birders
around the world. www.ebird.com.

National Audubon Society. Wonderful photos, up-to-the-minute facts
about conservation, and tips on how to observe and protect birds in
your own neighborhood. www.audubon.org.

World Wildlife Fund. Information about conservation efforts around
the globe. www.worldwildlife.org.

ACKNOWLEDGMENTS

Deepest thanks to my beloved agent, Sarah Davies, who's helped me hatch many a book, and to my wonderful editor, Margaret Ferguson, who gave this story its wings. Gratitude to Paul Sweet of the American Museum of Natural History for sharing his extensive knowledge of ornithology, and to copyeditor Janet Renard for dealing with the names of species and places both real and fictional. Many thanks to my brilliant flock of writer friends, especially Mary Grimm, Susan Grimm, Mary Norris, and Kris Ohlson. To all the generous, creative, tireless educators and librarians who work to connect kids and books: if I were a meadowlark, I would sing you my sweetest song! As always, to those who share my nest through good times and hard, I owe you everything.